Hana Rysová is from a small country in the middle of Europe. She began writing when she was ten years old and has continued to pursue her passion throughout middle and high school. Later, Hana studied creative writing at the University of Worcester, where she worked with her lecturer to publish a Christmas story on the library's website. Currently, she is working as a flight attendant and drawing inspiration from her life experiences for her stories.

Hana Rysová

GIRL FROM THE MIRROR

AUSTIN MACAULEY PUBLISHERS®

LONDON • CAMBRIDGE • NEW YORK • SHARJAH

A CIP catalogue record for this title is available from the British Library.

ISBN 9781035872480 (Paperback)
ISBN 9781035872497 (ePub e-book)

www.austinmacauley.com

First Published 2024
Austin Macauley Publishers Ltd®
1 Canada Square
Canary Wharf
London
E14 5AA

Chapter 1

The sun rose brightly and shone on the earth. People started their daily routines and followed familiar paths. On this usual day, something changed quietly. It was like a soft breeze. The people didn't notice. Fate brought excitement into their lives. As the clock ticked, she worked to get the restaurant ready for opening.

The restaurant in Worcester was cosy and well-lit. A young server named Crista discovered an old mirror that fascinated her. The mirror's worn frame and aged glass had a special charm. It drew her in, making time seem to stop. Crista gently ran her fingers over the detailed carvings on the mirror. She felt a connection to the many people who had looked at their reflections in it. When she saw her own reflection, she felt curious and amazed. It felt like she was in a world where the past and present were mixed. In this ordinary world of routines, a normal day went by.

Crista was just wiping the tables when she saw something strange in the mirror's reflection. Curious, she looked at the fancy-framed mirror. The reflection showed a beautiful person, not tired Crista. Her short blond hair was now long and brown. Her eyes were a captivating emerald green. After a short observation, it became clear that it wasn't Crista whose reflection was in the mirror.

The girl looked familiar to Crista. She struggled to remember their earlier meeting. It was clear that this person looked different. Their clothes were not like Crista's. Crista usually wore a white shirt and black pants. But today, she wore a bright green top and jacket. This was not typical. Crista was unsure about what the girl was wearing below her waist. It was a mystery. The picture only showed the top half of her body. The bottom half was hidden.

Crista was surprised by her reflection in the mirror. She dropped her cleaning cloth and gasped. She couldn't resist the urge. She touched the mirror's cold surface. A bright light flashed, lighting up the room. Suddenly, she found the girl tumbling out of the mirror as if through a magical portal.

The bright light made Crista close her eyes gently. The soft glow disappeared into the dark. The mirror girl used to be very beautiful. Now, she lay still on the cold floor. The girl's face was hidden by her long hair. But she couldn't look away from the girl. The girl wore a stunning outfit. She had on a green dress and a matching coat. The dress was even brighter than it looked before in the mirror.

Crista gently brushed away the strands of hair that obscured the young woman's face. She yearned to find whether the young girl's chest rose and fell in a rhythmic dance of life. She did so with bated breath. At that moment, Crista's gentle fingers touched her skin. She felt a strong sensation. A cold feeling, like ice, went through her skin, giving her shivers. Crista was confused and didn't know what to do. She tried to wake up the person in front of her quickly.

The girl took a deep breath before Crista touched the fragile girl. Her heart skipped a beat as she realised the girl was still alive, despite being unconscious. Crista felt vulnerable and uncertain. Tremors ran through her body, showing her inner turmoil. She knew she needed help and couldn't continue alone on this difficult path.

In a serious situation, she asked for help. Her plea echoed in the restaurant. It sounded urgent and hopeful. She hoped her co-workers would notice and help her. She wanted them to figure out what was wrong. A girl lay unconscious in front of them. Maybe one of her colleagues could wake her up.

Crista waited nervously for her friend to arrive. She tried to wake the sleeping girl many times, but it didn't work. Crista looked at the girl breathing in the dim room. In the darkness, this small hope stood out. It gave a bit of comfort. Crista was hesitant to help because she didn't know how.

Sabrina was carefully checking the drinks in the basement. Suddenly the dimly lit corridors echoed with Crista's desperate cries for help. The cries made Sabrina's heart race. She quickly went up the stairs with determination. Her heart pounded with each step. Sabrina sprinted towards Crista, who looked frightened. Crista stood frozen, her eyes wide with fear. Sabrina calmly took out her phone and dialled 999 for an ambulance. She turned up the volume so both she and Crista could hear everything clearly.

The dispatcher's voice echoed through the receiver, urging Sabrina to explain her situation. It was quick, considering how serious it was. The woman on the phone guided their actions calmly. She instructed them how to lay the girl. Crista carefully put the young girl in a safe position as she was instructed. They gently moved the girl to lie on her left side. She made sure the girl was comfortable and secure. Time seemed to slow down as she watched over her. She held the girl steadily.

They received explicit instructions, emphasising the urgency of the situation. It was made clear that if the ambulance didn't arrive within 30 minutes, they would do a critical procedure. They would gently shift the unconscious girl onto her opposite side. She was confident they would arrive on time. However, she didn't know the traffic conditions.

The problem started when the woman asked for the girl's name. No one knew the answer. Crista made a quick decision and announced her own name mere moments later. In a heartfelt manner, she further expressed that she bore the familial bond of being her sister. Sabrina's eyes widened in astonishment as she gazed at Crista. Surprised by the revelation, Crista found herself intrigued, her curiosity piqued. She didn't realise she wanted to stay connected to this mysterious woman. Enthralled by her presence, she found herself irresistibly drawn to unravel the depths of her being. She yearned to uncover the secrets hidden within.

Within a mere ten minutes, the piercing wail of an ambulance reached their ears. With a swift motion, Sabrina snatched the keys from their resting place on the back door. Her fingers closed around the cool metal. A sense of purpose filled her as she made her way outside, anticipation building in her chest. In the solitude of the room, Crista remained in the company of the young girl.

"Who are you?" She whispered in the girl's direction, "Why did you appear here, and where did you come from?"

Crista found herself caught in a web of uncertainty when it came to her feelings towards the girl. A peculiar sensation washed over her. A faint whisper of familiarity tickled her senses. There was an undeniable inkling that she knew this person. Yet, it stayed shrouded in an enigmatic haze. This left her with an uncanny, perplexing sentiment. It was like they had lost a friend from childhood or had known each other in a past life. Even if they didn't know each other, Crista still wanted to find out who they were.

The emergency team arrived on time. A loud knock echoed through the air. It carried a sense of urgency and came from the door. With a swift turn of the doorknob, Sabrina ushered in the presence of two men, their figures now gracing the room. They saw a young girl sprawled on the cold floor. Urgency gripped their hearts, and they hurried forward.

In the first moments, their attention was drawn to the vital signs of the young woman. Her breath, a gentle rise and fall, and the faint throb of a pulse beneath her skin. Following the earlier events, they proceeded to meticulously scrutinise her eyes.

"We will have to take her to the hospital, and she will need to have more tests done. Do you have her ID?" The tall man asked.

As Crista's response escaped her lips, a surge of urgency propelled her towards the staff area. With a determined stride, she navigated the labyrinthine corridors. Her mind was fixated on retrieving her personal belongings. The anticipation grew with each step, as she yearned to lay her hands on her own identification card.

Crista hurried back to the waiting paramedics, breathless and with a sense of urgency. Her heart pounded in her chest.

With a trembling hand, she extended her identification card. The man meticulously transcribed the intricate details onto their system. He ensured not a single element was overlooked. Once the task was completed, he gracefully returned the document to Crista. She was its rightful owner. In the midst of the scene, the second man gently hoisted the young girl onto the plush deckchair. He ensured her comfort as he patiently bided his time. He observed the first man's meticulous attention to the finer points. In unison, their collective strength propelled her towards the waiting ambulance.

"May I come with you? She is my sister, and I want to be with her," Crista said near the vehicle.

"Unfortunately, no, but we will be taking her to Worcestershire Royal Hospital. You should visit her there," responded one of the paramedics. The second one made their way towards the rear of the vehicle, accompanied by the young lady. Meanwhile, the first one took their position in the driver's seat. They securely shut the doors behind them. Then, they proceeded with purposeful strides towards the hospital. With a flick of a switch, the sirens blared to life.

Crista's gaze fixated upon the rear of the vehicle. The ambulance vanished around the bend. A surge of determination coursed through her veins. It compelled her to pursue their path. With a sense of urgency, she swiftly made her way back to the staff room. There, amidst the flurry of activity, she deftly retrieved her jacket and handbag. Without wasting a moment, she hastened towards her car. Her steps were purposeful and determined. Sabrina, driven by determination, made a valiant effort. She wanted to halt

Crista's progress. With a firm resolve, she confronted her, demanding nothing short of complete transparency.

"Why did you tell them she was your sister? Do you know the girl? What was she doing here? Where are you going?"

"We don't have time for this. Please tell the boss, I was feeling sick and left home. I will call you in the evening and answer all these questions." Crista asked before she left.

With a sense of urgency, she knew she had to move swiftly. Her car, her trusted companion, patiently awaited her in the vast expanse of the car park. Crista crossed a short distance. It seemed farther than usual to her at this hour. In the span of mere moments, though for her, it felt as if time had stretched into an interminable expanse. It was not unlike the passage of two arduous hours.

She was in profound disbelief. She found herself grappling with the simple task of opening her car's door. The shock that coursed through her being had rendered her hands unsteady. Her fingers trembled as they fumbled with the handle. After several valiant attempts, she finally achieved success. This granted her the privilege of proceeding directly to the esteemed hospital.

In the meantime, the ambulance arrived at the hospital. The paramedics brought the girl inside, where the nurse took over. As the doctors checked her, they decided to keep her in the hospital until she woke up. This was so they could perform a complex exam. The exam would determine what caused her unconsciousness. But the problem was that they didn't know when she would wake up. They also worried her unconscious state might cause harm.

Crista endured an interminable journey through the congested city streets. Finally, she arrived at the hallowed grounds of the hospital. The relentless traffic had conspired against her. It stretched the mere thirty minutes into an eternity of frustration and impatience. Nevertheless, she remained resolute, determined to fulfil her purpose within those sterile walls. Those thirty minutes stretched out before her like an eternity. Each passing second felt like an agonisingly slow heartbeat. Time stretched out endlessly before her, each passing moment feeling like an eternity. Yet, despite the weariness that settled in her bones, she persisted. The desire to unravel the mystery surrounding the girl consumed her. She felt determined to be there when the girl finally stirred from her slumber. It held a greater significance in her life than her mere occupation. She understood with unwavering certainty that safeguarding the young girl was her duty.

Gracefully manoeuvring her vehicle into an available spot, she deftly parked her car. Then, she swiftly made her way towards the entrance. As she approached, the receptionist warmly greeted her, extending a welcoming gesture.

"Hello, how can I help you?" The woman at the reception asked her.

"Hello, I want to visit Crista Smith. She was unconscious and should have arrived a few minutes ago," Crista said to her.

A woman looked at her computer and asked, "Well, and you are?"

"I am her sister, Amanda," Crista said, using her second name.

"She is currently being seen by the doctor. A nurse will tell you when you should visit her. Meanwhile, you can sit there," the woman said and pointed at the chairs in the corner of the room.

Crista expressed her gratitude and gracefully took a seat in one of the chairs. She spent the next few minutes hypnotising the door. She hoped that the nurse would appear and reveal information about the unknown girl.

After what felt like an eternity of waiting, Sabrina engaged in a seemingly endless series of phone conversations. Finally, the nurse uttered her name. Impatience coursed through Crista's veins, a restless energy that propelled her forward. The mere sound of her name was enough to ignite a spark within her. It prompted her to leap onto her chair with a sense of urgency. Without a second thought, she abandoned her jacket and handbag. She was forsaking the usual trappings of her daily routine. With single-minded determination, she sprinted towards the door. She was driven by a fervent desire to discover what awaited her on the other side. The nurse gently tapped her on the shoulder. It was a subtle reminder that she had left her belongings on the chair. Crista's cheeks flushed with a delicate pink. She gracefully retraced her steps to her belongings. She obediently trailed behind the nurse, with a sense of anticipation. Her footsteps echoed softly in the expansive hospital corridors.

The nurse led Crista through different corridors of the hospital. She could see people in the hallway who were walking the other way. She wondered what they were doing in the hospital. For Crista, it was very emotional. She would soon meet a girl whom she helped. She didn't know anything about her, but she felt a connection with her.

Nurse and Crista made their way down the corridor, their anticipation palpable in the air. The room they sought housed a mysterious girl; her identity was shrouded in secrecy. As they entered, their eyes fell upon her delicate form, resting upon the bed like a fragile flower. Her serene countenance belied the truth that lay beneath the surface. Though her eyes were closed, her visage held an ethereal beauty, as if she were merely lost in a peaceful slumber. Yet, the labyrinth of machines and intricate web of hoses enveloped her fragile form. They painted a starkly contrasting picture. She was also changed into the hospital's pyjamas.

"The doctor will be here in a minute," the nurse said before she left Crista alone in the room just with the girl.

"Hi, I hope you are alright," Crista whispered in the girl's direction. "I don't know why, but I feel like I know you from somewhere, but I'm not sure where. But I promise I will be here when you wake up."

Her desire to persist was abruptly interrupted. The door swung open, revealing a youthful male doctor.

"Hello, you have to be Amanda," the doctor said. Crista nodded. The doctor continued, "Your sister hit her head severely. The exams indicate that she may not remember anything before the accident. It is even possible that she will not remember you."

Crista's eyes widened in astonishment as she gazed at the doctor before her. Naturally, she had no memory of their previous meetings. Their paths hadn't crossed yet. She felt an urge to show her predicament to the esteemed doctor. However, she chose to maintain a composed silence instead. She offered a subtle nod of understanding.

"Do you know when she will wake up?" She asked instead.

"It will be in twenty-four hours, but we cannot promise anything."

"May I stay with her until she wakes up, please?"

"Well, we usually do not allow it; however, I believe we could do an exemption in your case. Would you like to contact your parents or any of your relatives?"

"No, we don't have anyone other than each other," Crista said honestly. She lived alone. Her parents died last year in a car crash, and she didn't have any other relatives.

The doctor just nodded and wrote it into the paperwork. Crista was glad he didn't ask more questions about it. After a few more checks, the doctor left the room and left Crista alone with the girl. Crista was glad that they believed her lies and didn't investigate it more closely.

Chapter 2

After the doctor's departure, Crista found herself in a modestly adorned chamber. The room had no extravagant embellishments. It had a singular bed, a sturdy wooden cupboard, a quaint table with two chairs, and a small bedside table. A solitary door beckoned from a discreet corner. Its purpose was concealed behind its unassuming facade. Crista carefully positioned one of the chairs near the bed. She made sure there was an unobstructed view of the girl. She found solace in the fact that the young girl had room for herself. She didn't know how she would react to her or another person. The young woman is surrounded by trepidation. Whispers of her potential danger fill the air.

Crista was unaware, but her insatiable curiosity compelled her to remain steadfastly by the woman's side.

Her gaze fell upon the calm face of the sleeping young woman. Her hair cascaded delicately around her face, framing her features like a halo. She possessed an undeniable charm. A petite nose and dainty lips completed the picture of her captivating allure. Curiosity enveloped her as she pondered the young woman's sexual orientation. She wondered if the woman was straight or gay. In addition, she found herself pondering how to communicate with her. Did the girl speak

English? Did they use a different language? Would she be able to understand her?

The girl didn't wake up for another three hours. Crista's concern for her well-being had been steadily growing during those long, silent hours. Eventually, Crista saw a small movement. It was just a movement of her fingers and her eyelid. It was very subtle movements, but they were there. Crista's posture became erect as she settled into her seat, her anticipation palpable. She patiently awaited the moment when the girl would finally unveil her eyes to the world. With bated breath. Crista's gaze fixated on the ceiling. Her emerald, green eyes beheld the expanse above her for the first time.

In those initial moments, the young girl's gaze fixated upon the obscure corner of the room. Confusion clouded her features. She grappled with the task of deciphering her surroundings. Crista exhibited remarkable patience towards her. She allowed herself plenty of time to get used to the new situation. Then, she took the first step by looking at herself in the mirror.

The girl took her time. Nearly ten minutes passed since she had woken up. As her gaze shifted, she started to observe the room around her. And then the girls' eyes met for the first time. Crista found herself captivated by the girl's eyes. They seemed to hold the vastness of the ocean within their depths. It was as if time itself stood still. She gazed into those mesmerising orbs. She longed to spend an eternity lost in their enchanting embrace.

"Ceeleste sesta?"[1] The girl uttered her first words since their captivating gaze. Crista found herself unsure of the language the girl was speaking.

"Hi, I am Crista." Crista tried to introduce herself. A flicker of hope danced within her. She yearned for a glimmer of recognition in the girl's eyes, a sign that they shared a common language. "How are you feeling?"

But at the same moment that Crista spoke, the girl's expression changed. She looked more confused than when she woke up, and it was clear that she didn't understand Crista.

"Do you speak English?" Crista tried one more time, hoping she would have luck and the girl would understand.

"Kovosto?"[2] Crista was forced to admit that the girl didn't speak the same language as her.

"Me," Crista pointed at herself, "Crista," then she pointed at the girl and said, "You?"

"Kenesta," she added, pointing to herself. Crista assumed that it was her name.

Crista was glad to find out her name. Now she was more worried about how she could communicate with the girl. If she didn't speak the same language, what about doctors and nurses? They would need to communicate with the girl.

◠◠◠

Kenesta opened her eyes. She didn't remember falling asleep or going to bed. The last thing she remembered was that she was with her family in the market to buy some vegetables for dinner. As her senses gradually awakened, Kenesta's attention turned to her surroundings. The room, she noted with certainty, was not her own. Its sterile ambience stood in stark contrast to the warmth and familiarity she was accustomed to. And then, her gaze fell upon a figure that seemed equally out of place. The girl had short blond hair and wore a funny thing on her face. It looked like another set of eyes.

Kenesta tried to hide her surprise and not laugh at the thing on the woman's face. Still, behind them, the girl had pretty green eyes. They were the exact same colour as the grass at her favourite clearance. The girl most likely knew what happened to her and where she was. She also probably knew something about her family.

"Ceeleste esta?"[1] Kenesta asked. She needed to know where she was. She needed to know it. But the girl in front of her spoke in a foreign language. Kenesta had never heard it said in the language before. It wasn't even similar to any language she heard during her travels around Olostia.

But again, the girl attempted to speak to her, but Kenesta was unable to understand her language. Kenesta told her in her speech to assure the girl that they didn't speak the same language. The girl watched her for a moment and then spoke again, but now she used her hands.

"Me," the girl said, pointing to herself; "Crista, you?" She asked, pointing to Kenesta.

It looked funny, but Kenesta figured out that the girl, no Crista, was introducing herself to her. Kenesta used the same way to say her name: by pointing at her own chest and saying her name, "Kenesta."

Kenesta wanted to sit up; she didn't like lying in bed. But she was weak, so she nearly tumbled from her resting place. Crista swiftly intervened, preventing her descent, and gently guiding her back onto the bed's surface. With a sense of purpose, Crista retrieved a diminutive box and deftly pressed a button. Kenesta was astonished when the bed sprang to life. It autonomously adjusted its position, elevating her to a more comfortable stance. For the first moment, she was shocked. She didn't expect anything like it. But Crista probably just used magic like his mother used to do.

"Better?" Crista asked her, but Kenesta didn't know what she said. She didn't respond as she was unable to understand.

Kenesta's gaze swept across the room, her eyes taking in the simplicity of its design. A pristine white canvas, devoid of any adornments, greeted her curious gaze. Positioned on the far side were two doors, standing as sentinels to an unknown realm beyond. She couldn't help but wonder which of these portals would grant her passage into the rest of the house. Yet, the presence of the second door remained an enigma. Its purpose was shrouded in mystery.

"Kelista, este si?"[3] Kenesta tried to ask Crista if she had anything to drink. She also used her hand to show her that she needed to drink, but Crista didn't seem to understand her. Kenesta was frustrated.

'There had to be some way to speak with her. I want to know more about this world, but…' Her thoughts were disturbed by another voice in her head.

"Who said that?" Kenesta was able to understand it.

"Telepathic, of course," Kenesta thought happily.

"What?" Crista sounded shocked. She didn't know where the other voice came from or why she heard it in her head.

"We can speak with our thoughts," Kenesta explained in her mind.

"Uh, okay I guess, how are you feeling?" Crista asked in her mind. She wasn't sure how this thing worked, but if it was their only chance to know each other, she would cooperate.

For Crista, it was weird to communicate with someone without speaking aloud. But Kenesta was used to this kind of communication. Sometimes she used to do it with her friends when they were unable to see each other. And she was also friends with vampires who spoke a different language. But she didn't know why she hadn't thought about it before.

"I'm feeling a little weak and thirsty," Kenesta replied. "Do you know where I can get some water or illusion[4]?"

"I will bring you some water or probably tea; don't worry." Crista stood up and left through one of the doors. For now, she left Kenesta alone in the room with her disturbing thoughts. She didn't have the chance to ask her where she was. Crista was too fast.

Kenesta was left alone and had to face the realities of her situation. She cast her gaze upon her physical form. She detected no visible wounds. Yet, an undeniable weakness permeated her being. Fatigue clung to her like a heavy cloak, while an unfamiliar emptiness gnawed at her core. It was like she had lost something very important.

Kenesta made the decision to meditate. With time on her hands until Crista's return, she might investigate what had happened. She emptied her head of any thoughts before following the emptiness. An ethereal allure enveloped her. She found herself irresistibly drawn into the depths of her own consciousness.

Kenesta materialised from the shadows, an enigmatic presence that defied the natural order. The peculiarity of her emergence in the darkness added an air of intrigue to the scene. This was where she normally saw her magical core. However, in the present moment, there occurred an absence of anything substantial. With determination, she ventured further into the depths. Her body sliced through the water with graceful strokes. Her goal was clear: to reach the very core.

However, to her surprise, she did not discover the grand treasure she had anticipated. Instead, she found a tiny, vibrant green sphere. The object in question possessed dimensions so diminutive that it could be likened to a mere pea. With a sense of helplessness, she could only watch her small core. This wasn't right.

"Sas!"[5] she exclaimed. This was impossible unless she exhausted her magic, but it never happened like this. She wanted to find out what happened to her magnificent core, but she didn't have enough time.

Kenesta woke up from her meditation session. It was enough for now; she would return later, hoping that things would be different. Her magic might return. But for now, she didn't know what to do with it. She appeared to have been exhausted during the journey to this location. It had to be far away if the core looked like this. Her mother had told her a similar tale. In that story, the person teleported to a different time. Was her experience the same? Or was it something else?

As Crista came back into the room, it looked like Kenesta was lost in thought. Crista was carrying a tray with a glass of water, a teapot with two cups, and a plate with food. Kenesta smiled at the small gesture Crista made for her. It was comforting to know that someone cared about her, despite the fact that they just met.

"I thought you might be hungry, so I got you some sandwiches from the cafeteria," Crista said. She smiled at her and put the tray on the bedside table.

"Kavaste,"[6] Kenesta thanked Crista, but she said it aloud, and Crista didn't know what she was saying.

"Sorry?" Crista asked her, confused.

"Sorry, I mean thank you," Kenesta said telepathically instead. Crista heard the words in her mind and understood.

"Could I ask what this place is?" Kenesta asked after a few minutes when she had eaten.

"Worcester, in the UK," Crista answered without hesitation.

"Where?" Kenesta didn't understand. She had never heard about the UK or Worcester.

"In England," Crista tried to specify in hope. Kenesta would know this name. But she still didn't get it.

Kenesta had no idea what these place names meant, and she was certain they were not in the Olostia.

"I get it. You still have no idea," Crista said.

"No, I've never heard of this country," Kenesta said, shaking her head.

"That's fine; I'll show you when they let you go," Crista said with a smile.

"And what is this place?"

"You are currently in the hospital because when I found you, you were unconscious."

"What is a hospital? Do you mean Kesistas[7]?"

"I don't know what Kasitat is. But the hospital is the place where you go when you don't feel healthy or you are hurt," Crista mispronounced the word Kenesta said. Kenesta wanted to ask more questions about this new place, but she was disturbed by a knock on the door. The door opened, and some kind of woman went in.

"Hello, I see you are awake. How are you feeling?" The woman said, but Kenesta stayed and looked confused.

"She's feeling good," Crista said. She made a mental note to translate everything after the nurse left.

"Did she speak with you?" The nurse asked.

"She tried, but she forgot how to speak," Crista answered quickly.

"That's odd," the nurse noted in the papers she was holding.

"Do you know when she could leave?" Crista asked her, and she hoped it would be soon.

"Well, we'll keep her here for observation until next week. If everything is fine, she can go," the nurse replied.

Neither the nurse nor Crista saw the confused look on Kenesta's face. Kenesta was trying to understand their conversation.

"May I stay with her?" Crista said she didn't feel comfortable leaving Kenesta in that place when she wasn't able to understand.

"Unfortunately, not; it is against our policies. You can stay here until the visitors' hours end. You can come back tomorrow at nine in the morning," the nurse informed her before leaving the room.

Crista turned back to Kenesta and finally saw her facial expression.

"I'm sorry, she was asking how you were feeling, I informed her that you are unable to speak. And I asked her if I could stay," Crista informed Kenesta via telepathy. Kenesta's face changed to one of hope when she mentioned staying in the hospital. But Crista said she couldn't stay with her during the night.

"Why can't you stay here?" Kenesta asked disappointedly.

"It's some kind of policy. I don't know exactly, but I will be back in the morning. I will start to teach you English so you can communicate with them," Crista said optimistically.

"Do you think it is a good idea?" Kenesta said this pessimistically. She didn't like the idea because, in Olostia, it was an insult to speak a language other than your mother tongue.

"Don't worry, it would be fine," Crista said without knowing why Kenesta didn't want to learn her language.

Kenesta disagreed with Crista. She was uncomfortable insulting this culture. She was new here, and now Crista wanted her to insult her culture, country, and language. Did she hate her? Crista stayed with Kenesta for another two hours when they tried to get to know each other. Crista wanted to begin teaching Kenesta some English words, but she refused. She was afraid of the insults, and Crista left her there. She was also scared that she could forget Okelestik's language, and that would make her lose her identity. Okelestika was part of Olostia. It was the part where Kenesta lived with her family and where she grew up.

Crista had reiterated on multiple occasions that such an occurrence was highly unlikely. She had made it clear that countless individuals can speak two or more languages. However, Kenesta obstinately disregarded her counsel. To her, another language meant mocking the country, and she didn't want that.

Crista decided to wait until another day. She would bring some books about multilingualism. She would also bring some workbooks for beginner language learners. She knew it would be hard to talk Kenesta into learning new languages, but she had to. Crista didn't know how to send Kenesta back or where she was from exactly.

After Crista left the hospital, she went to the Hive, the biggest library in Worcester. It was also the university library. She was sure that she would find the books there. The library is in the bustling city centre. Crista gracefully manoeuvred her vehicle through the labyrinthine streets. She eventually found a suitable spot to park. She alighted from her car. Then, she strode purposefully towards the library. Her anticipation was palpable in the crisp air.

Before going to the third floor, where there were academic and adult books, she bought a coffee in the library cafeteria. She knew it would be long hours of browsing through the shelves of text. She had been up since five o'clock in the morning. She was tired and needed sleep or coffee. She wanted to choose her bed and sleep, but she had to wait. For now, the coffee had to be enough to keep her from falling asleep while she found the books she needed.

With the coffee, Crista got a lift and went to the third floor. She turned right when the lift stopped. The shelves had academic books. The first few shelves were about learning the language. There were books to learn new languages. Books for multilinguists or non-native speakers could improve their English.

Crista searched in the section for more than an hour, but she could not find the books she wanted. One of them was for beginner learners. The book was written in English. Pictures were supposed to help learners with vocabulary. The book also included the English alphabet. Crista knew this book would help Kenesta with learning.

The second book was more about culture and language. There was a description of the importance of learning a foreign language. It also explained the identity of the speaker and how it could change during learning. But they also explained that the speaker didn't lose the ability to speak their mother tongue. It would decrease but not disappear. Crista hoped that this book would teach Kenesta that she didn't need to be scared of learning another language. The remaining books were all children's books for the first reading.

After Crista borrowed all the books, she went to buy some food for herself and then drove home. She arrived at her apartment house around eight o'clock. She wanted just her bed, but first, she rechecked her phone. There were some messages from her boss and Sabrina. Each was concerned about her well-being. The text messages from her boss asked if she would go back to work the next day. She knew she would have to go back because she needed money. Still, Crista could not leave her in the hospital alone for longer than necessary.

Hello, sorry, but I would need a holiday for at least two weeks. I know it is on short notice, but it is a family emergency. Thank you, Crista.

Crista wrote to her boss in the hope that he would understand. They have a good working relationship, and every time he needed something, she went to work.

That's fine; I hope everything will be alright. Let me know if you need anything.

She got an answer in less than two minutes. Crista was glad for the response; it meant she had time to care for Kenesta. After dinner, she went to bed. But she couldn't fall asleep. She looked for an app or website to help Kenesta with English.

ﷻ

On the other side of the city, Kenesta was bored. She wanted to do something, but she didn't know what. There weren't many options. She would love to read a book, but she wouldn't understand it. The nurses were coming in and out during the day, and they tried to speak with her, but she didn't know what they said.

One of the nurses brought a few sheets of paper. She probably hoped they would be able to communicate by writing. Kenesta had faith in it as well, but when she saw the text written in an unusual alphabet, she knew it wouldn't work. But the nurse left the papers there for Kenesta. She also brought some coloured pens. Kenesta grabbed one of the papers and pens. She started writing down her thoughts about this new world.

This world is strange. The language sometimes sounds funny. I would be glad to understand them without learning the language. But the girl, Crista, insisted that I have to learn. But the idea of speaking another language frightened me. In my home, it is an insult to the culture to learn their language. And this girl wants to teach me her language. It is wrong.

One notable aspect worth mentioning is the absence of Kesistas in their society. However, they compensate for this

Kenesta was writing on the piece of paper when one of the nurses came. The nurse was intrigued by the mysterious nature of Kenesta's writing. She couldn't resist the urge to catch a glimpse of the paper's contents. However, to her dismay, the symbols before her were nothing more than enigmatic hieroglyphs. They bore no resemblance to any familiar alphabet she had encountered before. This peculiar encounter only served to reinforce the nurse's belief. She was convinced that Kenesta existed within her own insular realm. She was unable to effectively communicate with the outside world. It seemed evident that she grappled with autism or some form of learning disability. Her sister had previously shared this. The nurse left the room, her mind swirling with these thoughts. She promptly recorded her observations in the detailed notes about Crista Smith.

ᚾᚾᚾ

The next day, Crista came to the room at nine o'clock. She went straight to Kenesta's room. Before arriving at the hospital, she stopped in the bakery. She bought some pastries for Kenesta. Crista hoped that Kenesta would like them. In addition to the pastries, she also carried a collection of books borrowed from the library. She also brought a selection of her own garments. She believed they would provide Kenesta with more comfortable attire. Yet, Crista knew that, once Kenesta left the hospital, they'd need a whole new wardrobe. New clothes, shoes, cosmetics, and an array of other items would need to be procured. Furthermore, Crista contemplated the need to transform one of her own rooms into a private sanctuary for Kenesta. She wanted to ensure her friend's much-deserved privacy.

After a brief contemplation, Crista realised the endeavour would cost a lot. Yet, she found solace in the fact that her financial resources were more than enough. She knew they could cover any potential costs. Crista started saving money when she was fifteen and had her first summer job. The money was for cosmetics or a new phone, but she didn't spend it. It was two years ago when she lost her parents and inherited a few hundred thousand pounds. She was able to find a place to live without jeopardising her family's heritage.

Crista gracefully made her way towards the room, her steps light and purposeful. As she entered, her eyes fell upon Kenesta, who was seated on her bed, engrossed in a task. A paper and pen lay before her, evidence of her diligent efforts. Crista couldn't help, but observe the graceful movements of Kenesta's hand. Kenesta inscribed words onto the paper, her focus unwavering.

"Hello, how are you feeling today?" Crista drew Kenesta's attention to her by using telepathy.

"Hello, it's better today," she said. Kenesta looked at her and smiled. She was glad that she wasn't alone anymore and that she could speak with Crista.

"I brought you some pastries from my favourite bakery. I hope you enjoy them," Crista said. She handed her a bag full of freshly baked pastries.

"Kavaste, i custe este!" exclaimed Kenesta. She ignored the way she spoke.

"Sorry?" Crista asked, confused because she was unable to understand her.

"Sorry, I mean thanks; I am starving," Kenesta corrected herself.

"Didn't they give you any food?" Crista asked me to disbelieve.

"They did, but it was disgusting," Kenesta answered when she unpacked the pastries and took a bite of one of them.

"Do you like it?"

Kenesta nodded with a full mouth. She really enjoyed the food Crista brought her. "What exactly is it?"

"The one you are eating is a croissant. There are also cinnamon rolls and chocolate rolls," Crista answered with a smile.

"Can you bring them tomorrow again, please?" Kenesta asked her.

"Of course," Crista said, smiling and nodding. She was glad; Kenesta liked them that much. She wanted another one the next day.

"I brought some books, so you could start learning English," Crista said after a few minutes of quiet.

"Must I?" Kenesta asked, unsure what to do.

"Yes, it would be easier for you to live here," Crista told her.

"But I want to go back home," Kenesta said stubbornly.

"I understand you. But until we find a way to send you back, this will help you communicate here," Crista continued.

"But I don't want to disrespect your culture," Kenesta argued. "Learning and using your language is offensive to you."

"No, it isn't. It's actually honouring the culture," Crista said. She described what she had learned from one of the books.

"How could this be honouring another culture when you try to speak their language? You are unable to speak the same way as the speaker. It is unnatural," Kenesta said hysterically.

"Trust me, it is absolutely natural. Everyone can speak more than one language. And we appreciate it when someone is trying to speak English. Otherwise, how can you communicate with other cultures if you don't speak the same language?" Crista asked.

"We used telepathy for communication," Kenesta said without thinking.

"Well, we can't use telepathy, and you won't be with me every second of the day," Crista shrugged, "so you have to learn my language."

"But…" Kenesta tried to disagree.

"No buts, you must, and I will assist you." This commitment was not solely made to Kenesta but also extended to Crista. She harboured a deep sense of connection to Kenesta.

Chapter 3

It had been almost a week since Kenesta started learning the English language. But she felt disappointed. The language was complicated, and she didn't make any progress. No matter how hard she tried, the vocabulary remained just out of reach. It slipped through her fingers like sand. Each try at pronunciation was a dance of stumbling syllables. It was a symphony of missteps. Crista was patient with her, but Kenesta still felt terrible for her. She felt ashamed for messing with her language.

Every day, they persisted. Crista arrived with a collection of books. They were curated for those seeking to enhance their English skills. The books had charming illustrations. They were carefully made to captivate the young minds of the children who were just starting to learn a second language. However, to Kenesta's dismay, this book was not much help. She found herself unable to identify several of the images in it. In contemplating the essence of an apple, one is compelled to ponder its very nature. What, indeed, is an apple? It looked funny, and when she asked Crista, she left Kenesta for half an hour.

Upon her return, she triumphantly presented two apples. This evoked a sense of intrigue and amusement. She had a twinkle in her eye. She described the juicy bits as nothing less than nature's sweetest treasures. Kenesta was thinking about foods from her world when she bit one. It was hard, and she could taste sweet liquid coming out of the bite. It was actually tasty, and Crista said that it was healthy. After that day, Crista brought apples with her every morning.

Kenesta was released from the hospital that day and she was excited to see this new world. But she knew she needed to find a way home. In the realm of oddities and uncertainties, this world had taken on an eerie and disconcerting look. Longing for the comfort of her own abode, she yearned to return to the sanctuary of home. In her familiar realm, familiarity was supreme. It left no room for astonishment.

Also, she was deeply reluctant to impose on Crista. Crista insisted on hosting her. She would do so happily until they found a solution or until Kenesta learned English.

Kenesta was supposed to leave at ten o'clock. Crista decided to come just before Kenesta left. This meant that when Kenesta stepped out of the hospital building, no one was waiting for her. Crista arrived ten minutes late. She came in a strange metal box that looked like a carriage without horses. Crista was inside when she stopped it.

A wave of horror washed over Kenesta as she laid her eyes upon the vehicle. The object before them bore a striking resemblance to a coffin. Its sleek and sombre exterior cast an eerie shadow over the room. One couldn't help but wonder about the intentions behind its creation. This was the notion that Crista harboured a sinister desire to harm Kenesta. This notion was especially within it.

"Come in, Kenesta," Crista's voice said in her head. But Kenesta shook her head and stepped back from the coffin. The thought of her own demise was an unwelcome presence in her mind.

"No, no, no," she repeated, looking at Crista.

"Don't worry, nothing bad will happen to you," Crista tried to reassure her, but Kenesta refused to enter.

"Please, Kenesta, we don't have much time. We need to go to Ikea and buy you a bed. Then we need to go to Primark and buy you some clothes. Please come in so we can go," Crista said calmly.

"No, I don't want to die," Kenesta said, panicking.

"You won't die, not today, I promise," Crista said. It still didn't help. Kenesta's heart raced with anxiety as she gazed upon the ominous coffin before her. The mere thought of stepping foot into this peculiar object sent shivers down her spine.

Crista emerged from the strange contraption. She made her way to the enchanting realm of Kenesta. With a swift motion, she clasped both of her hands and locked her gaze into the depths of her own eyes.

"Do you trust me?" She asked Kenesta. Kenesta nodded.

"Okay, so just follow me," Crista said. Her lips curved into a gentle smile as she gracefully guided Kenesta to the awaiting vehicle. Kenesta followed her. She moved slowly. Her slowness matched the languid pace of the moment. They stood near the passenger door. Crista gracefully extended her hand to open it.

"Trust me, alright," she said, pushing Kenesta to the seat and closing the door. After that, she grabbed a bag that Kenesta had dropped after she started panicking and put it in the trunk. After that, she went to the driver's seat. But before they could go, Crista helped Kenesta with the seatbelt.

When Crista drove around the building, she saw some people who watched them curiously. It was probably because of the scene.

Kenesta remained seated, her gaze fixed upon the passing scenery beyond the window. She observed the unfolding journey with calm stillness. Her presence was a silent testament to her contemplative nature. She trembled with fear. She couldn't help but fear that the cold, unyielding metal box would become their prison. However, Crista deftly and meticulously handled the metal contraption. This managed to soothe her anxieties. It allowed calm to wash over her. As the minutes ticked by, Kenesta found herself growing calm. The cityscape was once bustling. It had towering buildings. It became a captivating sight through the windowpane.

In an unexpected turn of events, she even began to enjoy this dull task. Her current surroundings were different from her home. The difference was striking. Crista was in the vehicle. She deftly moved her fingers to press a button. This started a symphony of soothing melodies that filled the air. The tranquil notes danced lightly. They cast a spell of calm on the air. It was as if they made a peaceful sanctuary in the chaos outside. Kenesta was perplexed by the new word from the singer's lips. Yet, she found herself drawn to the enchanting melody that came with it.

"What kind of music is it?" Kenesta asked after a few moments of listening.

"Well, I am not exactly sure. It's something from the radio station," Crista answered.

"Radio station?" Kenesta didn't understand, as they didn't have anything like that back in her world.

"Yes, they play some songs every day and tell news from the country," Crista tried to explain.

"Oh, so you don't need to ask sirens to sing for you," Kenesta said, surprised. She usually had to go to the sea and ask some sirens to sing for her. Others could not keep the melody, or their song sounded like scratching.

"Ask sirens?" Crista didn't understand. Why would she need to ask sirens to sing for her?

"No, you don't need to ask the sirens. In this world, we have singers and musicians. They write their songs and then play them on the radio or on Spotify," Crista explained. But Kenesta looked shocked, and she didn't know what Spotify was or what a musician was.

"I'll show you when we get home," Crista said to end the discussion. She didn't want Kenesta to feel bad if she didn't know something.

Kenesta's head bobbed in agreement, her eyes fixating on the radio with a newfound focus. Her heart was wrapped in the enchanting allure of music. It was a passion that flowed through her like a symphony. Alas, the heavens had given her a voice. However, it did not meet others' high expectations. Whispers of doubt and discouragement echoed in her ears. They constantly reminded her of her perceived inability to sing.

For the rest of their journey, a hush settled between them. It was broken only by the soft songs from the radio. The melodies shifted and swayed as if dancing to an invisible rhythm. Occasionally, a voice would interject, punctuating the air with its presence. Kenesta was perplexed. She couldn't grasp the meaning behind the words of the mysterious figure in the box. She was reluctant to seek clarification. So, she chose to remain silent. This allowed her curiosity to simmer in her mind. Deep down, she felt like a heavy burden on Crista. Alas, she found herself at a loss. She was utterly clueless about how to change this sad reality. Kenesta yearned to learn Crista's language urgently. She longed to convey her emotions through words, not rely on telepathy.

Kenesta had never experienced the intoxicating depths of love quite like this. It was as if a symphony of feelings had erupted in her. Crista's captivating gaze had orchestrated it. In those eyes, she found a reflection of her soul. It was a deep connection that whispered of a destined union. The eyes before her exuded an undeniable kindness. They brimmed with an abundance of compassion that seemed to overflow. Was Crista also fond of her? For what other reason could she possibly be extending her assistance to her? Kenesta found herself adrift in a sea of thought. Her mind was consumed by a whirlwind. She didn't know it, but the world around her faded. She neglected to heed it.

Meanwhile, Crista parked the vehicle outside of the enormous building. There were signs, but Kenesta still didn't understand this world's alphabet, and she couldn't read it. Both got out of the vehicle and went inside the building. If the building was huge outside, inside it was enormous. There was furniture everywhere. This was honestly the strangest place Kenesta had ever been.

"We are here for just a few things, and then we will leave," Crista said, leading Kenesta in one of the many ways. It was like a prison maze, designed so people might never leave. She even grabbed a big basket on the wheel. Kenesta was impressed by all the stuff. Everything was in multiple colours or with different motives. She wasn't used to it.

Everything in the home was the same. Unlike this one, all of the pillows were the same colour or shape. Meanwhile, Crista was filling the basket with cushions and candles.

"Do you like anything?" Crista asked Kenesta when she saw her look at the small bookcase.

"Yeah, these shelves looked nice. It would be great to have a home for all my books," Kenesta answered. She spoke the words into Crista's mind. Crista felt them with the same jolt of amazement each time. Kenesta was looking in the same direction; imagine all her books from home. It was a small wooden shelf with square spaces. Kenesta loved the idea of the small shelf for manuscripts, but she also knew that she would never go back.

Crista didn't wait and wrote the serial number on a piece of paper. With resolve, she chose to get the item. It was destined for Kenesta's room. It is quite likely that such an action would bring her great joy. Crista diligently gathered all the things that would surely captivate Kenesta's interest. Her desire was for Kenesta to evoke a profound sense of belonging as if it were her very own sanctuary. Crista possessed limited knowledge about the mysterious individual. Throughout the week, they had talked. But Kenesta had stayed quiet about sharing details about her world. It possessed an air of forbidden allure, akin to a whispered secret that dared not be spoken aloud.

The shopping for furniture was quick, and the girls went to pay for all the stuff Crista put in the trolley. After that, they went back to the car, and Crista drove back to the city centre. First, she wanted to go to Birmingham because there were more shops there than in Worcester. However, she chose

Worcester. It should be easier for Kenesta to integrate than Birmingham's big, grand shops.

Shopping for clothes was far more enjoyable than shopping for furniture. Kenesta tried many shirt, top, and trouser styles. She tried them before she picked one. The sheer multitude of clothing options left her utterly astounded. And so, she left. She had many tops and a modest collection of dresses. She also had a few trousers and a pair or two, perhaps three, jackets. There were two cosy hoodies, three shoe sets, and some undergarments. Crista marvelled at Kenesta's transformation. Once otherworldly being now looked like an ordinary human woman.

"I think we could also go shopping next week," Crista said on the way to her house.

"Yeah, this was fun. I've never seen so many clothes in one place," Kenesta agreed. For her, this has been a nice day since she got there.

"Do you think we could try to teach you English?" Crista asked.

"Yeah, probably, but I don't want you to be disappointed," Kenesta said hesitantly.

"Don't worry; learning a language is not easy, and you will not disappoint me," Crista said supportively.

"All right," Kenesta said, nodding. She still wasn't ready to learn the language. Still, she wanted to show Crista that she appreciated her help with adaptation to this world.

"Good, could we start with greetings?" Crista asked.

"Yeah, but could it wait until we are out of this thing?" Kenesta tried to delay the language lesson.

"Yeah, that is a good idea, and we could also start with your writing," Crista decided.

Kenesta stayed quiet, but her expression showed she was not a fan of that idea.

Crista stopped the car in front of a large building where she had rented a flat. Both girls grabbed some bags with clothes or decorations, and Crista led them to the entrance. In the building, she went up the stairs to the third floor. She wanted to use a lift, but she didn't want to scare Kenesta with new things and explain them.

They stepped into the modest flat, its atmosphere tinged with a sense of familiarity. Crista gracefully guided Kenesta through the narrow hallway. She led them to the heart of the home: the living room. With a purposeful stride, she walked towards the refreshments. A delightful mix of drinks awaited her. Nearby, a collection of books beckoned. Their pages were filled with untold stories and hidden treasures. Kenesta cast her gaze about the room. Her sharp eyes were at once captured by the beautiful decor that adorned the flat. Nestled within the urban landscape, there existed a diminutive yet inviting abode. It had a small space. It had two bedrooms, a modest living space, and a quaint kitchen. Kenesta found herself standing before another room, its purpose shrouded in uncertainty. She thought it was a bathroom. But doubt lingered in her mind. It casts a veil of ambiguity over her assumption. The setting ought to mirror that of a hospital.

For the first time, Kenesta had used the bathroom in the hospital, and she was sceptical for she had never before availed herself of its facilities. Doubt lingered in her mind, casting a shadow of uncertainty over her every step. The unfamiliarity of the shower and the act of flushing toilets were foreign concepts to her. She lived in a quaint realm. A garden graced their home. It had a small lake that added serenity. As for the bathroom, it was hidden in the foliage. It was a small hole hidden by a curtain of trees. As her eyes beheld the miraculous sight of the self-cleaning toilet, a wave of relief washed over her. She would no longer have to scrub away yesterday's indulgences. And as if that weren't enough, the realisation dawned upon her that the shower, too, had shed its need for a warm spell. She would no longer have to endure the chilling embrace of frigid water. She would not have to endure it until it reached the desired temperature. At that moment, gratitude filled her heart. These small conveniences had made her daily routine easier and more enjoyable. Sometimes, she felt discontent. It would wash over her when she had to clean her body at her home. However, she had a new realisation. It showed the existence of another option. The level of comfort experienced was significantly higher.

Kenesta entered the living room. It was spacious and adorned with two plush sofas and a dainty table nestled between them. Also, one could find shelves covered with a variety of books. Their spines were neatly aligned in a symphony of knowledge. It was nestled in the corner. A strong presence came from a big black box. Its mysterious allure called curious minds to explore its secrets. Kenesta was filled with a sense of intrigue as she gazed upon the mysterious object before her. Its purpose eluded her. It left her with a burning curiosity. Only Crista's arrival could quench it. Patience became her ally. She eagerly awaited Crista's entrance into the room. Only then would the enigma be unravelled.

Gracefully, she settled onto one of the seating areas. She sank into the embrace of a luxuriously long, exquisitely cushioned chair. Kenesta sank into the plush fabric, feeling the tension melt away from her body.

Crista brought two glasses of water and put them on the small table. After that, she two books from the shelves and sat on the second sofa. Kenesta knew the books because Crista had been teaching her from them the whole week.

"Are you sure?" Kenesta asked one more time. She didn't like these lessons.

"Yes, you need it," Crista said strictly. "Where do you want to start?"

"Can we start with the alphabet, please?" Kenesta felt resigned.

Crista nodded and reached for one of the books. She opened it on the page with the English alphabet and put it in front of Kenesta.

"Do you remember any of it?" Crista asked her when she pointed at the letters.

Kenesta looked at the strange symbols. She wasn't sure if she remembered any of it, but she tried. She pointed at the letter with two big semicircles.

"B?" Kenesta said aloud.

"Yes," Crista said, nodding. "What about this?" Crista pointed at a similar symbol. It had just one semicircle ending in the middle of the line.

"D?" Kenesta attempted but was unsure.

"No, it's P. This is D," Crista said, pointing to a similar letter with a circle in the middle of the line.

"It's difficult," Kenesta sighed, frustrated.

"It's not. You just have to try. Try this one," Crista suggested, pointing to another letter in the shape of a roof with a line in the middle.

"A," Kenesta said with concentration. She tried to make Crista proud.

"Yes," Crista said, nodding and pointing to another.

They continued with the letters for another hour. Kenesta was able to recognise most of them, but she had a problem with similar letters like M and N, P and D, and G and C.

"Do you want to try to write your name?" Crista asked her with a smile of encouragement.

Kenesta just nodded. She was curious about the way her name would look in this strange alphabet. Crista stood up and went to fetch a piece of paper and a pen. She was glad that Kenesta wanted to try this. She was afraid to ask after the breakdown at the beginning, but now she saw that Kenesta wished to learn.

Crista came back with a few sheets of paper and two pens. She sat back at her place and put the papers in front of Kenesta. She grabbed them and started to imitate the symbols' shapes. Crista watched her, and she could see that Kenesta was enjoying writing or trying to write.

When Kenesta finished, she put the paper back and showed it to Crista. Crista was impressed by the words that Kenesta wrote. It was definitely her name, but Crista didn't know it was written as she pronounced it.

"Bravo!" Crista smiled at her. "Do you want to try my name?"

Kenesta nodded enthusiastically and grabbed the pen and paper again. Kenesta didn't know how to write Crista's name correctly, but she tried, and then she showed it to her. Kisda was written on the paper.

"Almost," Crista smiled, grabbed the second pen and showed her the proper way to spell her name.

"Sorry, I didn't know it is spelt differently than it sounds," Kenesta said in her mind. She apologised for her mistake.

"Don't worry. You can't know this. And you wrote it phonetically," Crista said calmly back, so the words rang in Kenesta's mind like tiny bells.

"Okay," Kenesta nodded but was feeling disappointed in her mistakes. She wanted to show Crista she could do it.

"Can we continue with English?" Crista asked out loud, and Kenesta just nodded. She didn't want to, but she had to.

"Good, can you say, please, Hello, I am Kenesta," Crista said.

"Hell, Aj em Kenesta," Kenesta attempted to imitate Crista's accent.

"It's almost like saying, Hello."

"Hello," Kenesta tried once more; she didn't like it. She was just trying to get Crista not to disappoint her and to be able to speak about her feelings through her voice.

"It was better," Crista said, smiling at her. She knew it would be hard. This was especially true after a week. Kenesta didn't improve her pronunciation or vocabulary. The rest of the day, they recapitulated the vocabulary from last week and tried to learn a few more. In between, they watched films and went for walks. Crista was glad she had taken time off work because she wanted to spend every moment with Kenesta. Idly, she wondered about the magic mirror.

On the same day, Crista introduced Kenesta to television. It is a captivating medium. It showcased a cinematic masterpiece in English, with subtitles. Alas, Kenesta couldn't understand the film. The words failed to bring her solace. Still, she found solace in the movie's pure entertainment. It offered a tantalising glimpse into this world's rich culture.

Around nine o'clock, Crista showed Kenesta her bedroom. It was her old office. During the week, Kenesta was in the hospital, she rebuilt the room into a cosy bedroom with a bed, table, armchair, and wardrobe. There would also be shelves for books in a few days, which they bought that day. Kenesta fell in love with the room immediately. It was more than her room in her home.

With a weary yet grateful smile, Kenesta acknowledged Crista's efforts. She expressed her heartfelt appreciation for the kindness being shown to her.

"No problem; the bathroom is behind that door if you want to use it before going to sleep. There's one more towel for you," Crista said. She pointed to the door. Kenesta had already assumed it was for the bathroom.

"No, I washed already this week, but thanks," Kenesta said, closing the door in front of a shocked Crista. The encounter had left her perplexed, unsure of how to process the situation. You see, Crista was accustomed to indulging in a daily shower, a ritual she held dear. However, Kenesta appeared to have different bathing habits. This fact piqued Crista's curiosity. Perhaps she thought it would be worthwhile to talk to Kenesta. They could discuss the intriguing differences in their routines.

The following day, they met in the kitchen. Crista had made some breakfast for them both. She made scrambled eggs with bacon and beans and some toast. She decided to prepare a real British breakfast to welcome Kenesta to her new house. She also prepared coffee and tea, so Kenesta could choose what she wanted.

Kenesta woke up around nine. She was surprised by the amount of sleep she got that night. She'd only slept a few hours since arriving in this world. That night she slept for at least ten hours. She felt relaxed and ready for the new day. After she changed, she went to the kitchen, where she found Crista with breakfast ready.

The amount of food was surprising for Kenesta, but she didn't complain. She was as hungry as a vampire. She sat at the table and started to eat. Meanwhile, Crista observed her with a steaming cup of coffee in hand. She was content knowing that Kenesta was enjoying her morning meal. However, Crista found herself grappling with the delicate matter. She had to broach the topic of Kenesta's personal hygiene habits.

"Kenesta, can we speak about something?" Crista tried slowly.

"Hmm, but if it's about English, should it wait until after the food?" Kenesta answered.

"No, it's about something else," Crista said.

"Well, I guess we can," Kenesta said nervously.

"It's actually about your hygiene," Crista said. She really didn't want to speak about it, but it was bothering her the whole night, and she needed to know why.

"What about it?" Kenesta was perplexed. She simply couldn't understand. After all, she washed every week. Her mother had instilled this habit in her. It had always been that way, an unwavering tradition. No one dared to wash more often, for the scarcity of warm water made it an arduous task to sustain.

"Well, I just wanted to ask how it is with the washing in your world. You should be disgusting to someone if you say you've already washed for this week."

"Disgusting? Why? The hot water needs maintenance. It is hard, so we wash just once a week to keep us clean without using the water," Kenesta said, surprising them.

"You know, here, we wash every day or at least every other day."

"And what about hot water?"

"We have boilers that heat the water and have it ready when we go to the shower or bath."

"So, you don't need a heating charm. Also, make sure there is enough time to clean the water after the bath," Kenesta didn't understand this stuff. She was confused.

Crista nodded, "Yeah."

"Great," Kenesta smiled, "but I still don't understand why showering once a week should be disgusting."

"Well, it should be because of smell or dirt. Or because you sometimes have an infection in your private areas," Crista tried to explain.

"Ok, I should probably try to wash more often, but I don't promise anything," Kenesta said. She didn't want any discussion about her parties.

"Thank you," Crista said.

Kenesta set down the cutlery. Her appetite vanished into thin air. The talk she had with Crista had just ended. It had left her feeling more inadequate than ever. She had expected to encounter different customs and practices in this foreign land. But the stark contrast she had just seen had caught her completely off guard. It left her pondering a myriad of questions. Were her seating arrangements appropriate? Was she eating with proper decorum? Did she follow the expected etiquette? Or were there additional nuances that she had yet to grasp?

"Did you finish?" Crista asked when she saw that Kenesta didn't eat anymore.

"Yeah," Kenesta admitted, embarrassed.

"What do you want to do now?" Crista asked her in the hope that they could continue learning English.

"Should we probably speak about rules and manners in this world? I don't want to offend anyone else in the future," Kenesta asked.

"Yeah, of course. Do you want to speak about it in the living room?" Crista asked. She wanted to help her so much, and she knew that Kenesta would not offend anyone else.

"Yes, please," Kenesta said. But before they moved to the living room, Crista poured another mug of coffee for Kenesta. She grabbed her phone to show her some examples of the world.

Kenesta sat on the plush sofas in the living room. Their hands delicately cradled the warmth from their mugs. A strong unease settled upon them. The conversation that was about to happen made her uncomfortable. She hated needing to ask about the differences in this strange place. Her heart yearned to return to her own world. Her loved ones and cherished companions lived there. The present circumstances felt like a waking nightmare. It was a disconcerting reality that she longed to escape. In her mind, she saw herself entering the green depths of the forest. She was with her dearest confidante, Kolusa. They shared tales and laughter in blissful abandon. Alas, the recollection of this cherished dream momentarily slipped from her grasp, replaced by the harsh reality of her situation.

"So, what do you want to know?" Crista asked her when she saw that Kenesta didn't start.

"Well, everything—holidays, religious practices, and so on."

"Ok, we have a couple of religions; the most important are Christianity, Islam, and Judaism. These three world religions are on a similar basis," Crista said eloquently. She was starting an enlightening talk. It was about the differences that set apart these three spiritual beliefs. She presented a collection of religious images to her. Kenesta tried to grasp all of Crista's words. Her mind worked to understand each one. In her quest for knowledge and understanding, she had a curious nature. It compelled her to ask whenever she found unfamiliar territory. She also asked when she wanted to delve deeper into a subject.

The religion lecture was long, over two hours. After that, Crista had to start making lunch for both of them. Kenesta helped her in the kitchen and asked a question about the electricity and how it worked.

After lunch, they continued the conversation about the world. Kenesta learned a lot of new stuff. She had no idea there would be so many different religious traditions. In her world, they had just the goddess Klistia, who was also the mother of the planet. And there were many other gods. Another surprise was Christmas; giving a gift one day per year sounded horrific. She was used to getting a gift for her friends at least once a week. She loved her friends, and she would do everything for them.

Crista asked some questions about Kenesta's world because she was curious about it. Kenesta had to describe to her the different species that lived there. It was fun, but Kenesta felt sad after all the remembering of her previous life. She wanted to be back.

When Kenesta went to her room during the afternoon, a weariness settled upon her, not of the physical kind, but rather a deep mental exhaustion. She reclined on the soft bed. She surrendered to the weight of her sorrow. Tears cascaded down her cheeks. She missed her home so much.

Crista stood behind the door to Kenesta's room and listened to her. It broke her heart. She knew she had to find a way back to Kenesta's world. She didn't want it because she felt connected to her and thought she was falling for her. She hadn't felt it for this long, but she knew it was real. As a result, she didn't want to hear about Kenesta's struggles in this world. She was aware that this world was crucial.

For two hours, Kenesta reclined on her bed, wrapped in soft sheets. After an hour, her tears were gone. She was unable to weep. Yet, she remained trapped in the labyrinth of her mind. Memories of her beloved parents, cherished siblings, and loyal friends held sway.

Kenesta found herself at home, accompanied by her younger sister, Elisita. She was three years younger than Kenesta. Kenesta had a strong connection with her. It was a relationship that held a special place in Kenesta's heart, one that she cherished deeply. In fact, Kenesta found herself devoting most of her rare free moments to this loved person. Their understanding of one another surpassed that of their fellow siblings. In a vulnerable moment, Kenesta confided in Elisita. She revealed her love for female creatures. To her relief, Elisita received this revelation with open-mindedness and acceptance.

In their quiet bedroom, Kenesta and Elisita sat side by side. Their delicate fingers gently glided through their lustrous hair. Soft sunlight filtered through the window. It cast a warm glow on their faces. They indulged in this simple act of self-care. Kenesta found great pleasure in the art of adorning Elisita's hair. Her hair cascaded down her shoulders, a silky waterfall of ebony strands. Each tress seemed to gleam with a lustrous sheen, reflecting the light in a mesmerising dance. The touch of her hair sent shivers down Kenesta's spine, a delightful sensation that sparked a warmth within her.

"Have you ever considered who your soulmate could be?" Elisita asked her.

"No, but I hope it would be a female, and she would treat me as a treasure. She would be kind and would help me during a hard time," Kenesta said of her dream partner. She didn't want someone who looked good but was a moron. She desired a clever, carrying creature. "Did you think about it?"

"No, but your idea sounds great. I hope mine will be the same," Elisita said.

"You deserve someone who would treat you with kindness," Kenesta said with a smile.

"Kavaste."

"You are welcome," Kenesta said. "Do you want to go to the lake?"

"Yes, we can swim, and probably there would be some sirens so they could sing some of their songs," Elisita agreed. She loved going to the lake.

"Great, grab towels, and we're ready to go," Kenesta said after finishing her sister's hair. Her sister stood up and put towels in the cupboard.

The girls went the shortest way to the lake. It was in the middle of the forest, where they lived. Kenesta loved every trip to the lake, and sometimes she wished to be a siren so she could just swim and sing.

In mere minutes, their footsteps led them to the lake. It embraced them with tranquil, shimmering waters. As if guided by an invisible hand, they gave in to the allure. The allure was irresistible and was of the aqueous sanctuary. With a fleeting break, they shed their boring clothes. They put on the vibrant garb of swimsuits. They promised freedom and water fun. Kenesta was the first to dash towards the tranquil expanse of the lake. The longing for the water was palpable within her.

"Hey, wait for me," Elisita called to her sister, and in a few seconds, she joined her in the lake.

"Kenesta, are you alright?" Kenesta heard Crista's voice in her mind. This disturbed her memory.

But Kenesta didn't want to answer her. She didn't feel okay and didn't want to talk with her. She was one of the problems, which is why she was stacked here, in this place without magic and without her family.

"Please answer me. I am worried about you," Crista continued, but Kenesta ignored her.

"Fine, if you want it this way, I am going inside," Crista said before opening the door to Kenesta's room. There she saw Kenesta lying in bed with puffy eyes from crying. Crista couldn't stand the look and went near Kenesta, where she sat on her bed. She then snatched her tight hug.

"Shh, it will be fine. I know how you're feeling."

"How?"

"I lost my family one year ago and still miss them."

"I'm sorry."

"You don't need to be. I promise we'll find a way to your house together."

"Thank you."

"No problem. Do you want to tell me more about your family or do you want to go on a walk?"

"Probably the walk, please, if it's alright."

"Sure, just go to the change and we can go." Crista nodded and stood up. She went to her room to change her trousers to jeans, grabbed a jacket and shoes, and waited in the hall for Kenesta. It took her more time than Crista, but they were ready and went on the walk after half an hour.

Crista led them to the park along the riverside. Kenesta enjoyed seeing nature, which was similar to her home. And she loved the river, but Crista didn't allow her to swim there. During their time outside, they saw sunshine. Kenesta was amazed by the beauty of the sky.

Back home, Crista ordered two pizzas for dinner. She didn't feel like cooking and didn't know if Kenesta knew how to cook.

"Do you want to take a shower? It sometimes helps to calm down," Crista offered to Kenesta.

"I believe so," Kenesta said, nodding. She went to her room and grabbed a towel and clothes to change into after.

Crista's gaze was fixed upon her, observing every subtle movement and expression. She remained uncertain about the course of action to take. She yearned to lend a hand yet found herself at a loss for a suitable course of action. Kenesta gracefully made her way to the bathroom. She gently closed the door behind her to create privacy and seclusion. Meanwhile, Crista subtly shifted her attention. She pivoted around and luckily stumbled upon her misplaced phone as if it had been waiting for her. She yearned for an extended break. She mustered the courage to dial her boss's number. Her heart pounded with anticipation. The notion of a long holiday had been swirling in her mind. She desired to bask in the luxury of time that surpassed any previous trip. It was clear that he was very displeased. He had no plans to grant her request for more holidays. The reason behind his reluctance was painfully clear. He had too few staff. They made him unable to accommodate her need for rest. However, after a series of heated debates, he reluctantly agreed to grant her more time. But she had to do more hours after she returned.

Kenesta emerged from the confines of the bathroom, her countenance noticeably transformed. Only ten minutes had passed. They had brought a big change upon her. It was as if stepping away had given her a new calm.

"Pizza will be here in a few minutes. Do you want chamomile tea?" Crista asked her when she joined her in the living room.

"Yeah, thanks," she nodded. Crista stood up and went to prepare a cup of chamomile tea for both of them. With two cups, she went back to the living room.

"Should we continue with English today?" Kenesta asked after a few minutes of silence.

"Yeah, of course," Crista said, nodding, surprised by Kenesta's wish. She had never attempted to learn the language on her own. This was the first time and should be a good sign.

"Do you remember greetings?" Crista started.

"Hello," Kenesta said aloud. She said it with confidence and the right pronunciation.

"Perfect, is there any other way?"

"Hi?"

"Yes, and something more polite?"

"Goood mornin'?"

"Almost, but yes, when do you use this one?"

"In the morning."

"Yes, is there an afternoon greeting?"

"Goood aftnun?"

"You are almost there, Bravo."

Kenesta tried one of the new words she had learned the day before, "Fanks."

Crista's gaze fixated on her. Her eyes didn't blink. It was as if she was searching for something profound. Then, without warning, her hands came together in applause. They filled the room with a symphony of admiration. Never before had Kenesta ventured into such uncharted territory. However, just as Crista was about to utter a word, the courier arrived with pizzas.

"I will be back in a few seconds," Crista said, and she went down to pick up pizzas from the courier. She used a lift to go downstairs. She grabbed both boxes from the courier and went back upstairs. Kenesta had never had pizza, and this was her first time. Crista was excited about what she had said.

Crista returned to the flat and gave one of the boxes to Kenesta, who carefully opened it. She was surprised by the shape. She had not anticipated circle food. It actually looked like one of the pies her mom used to make. But this looked salted, not sweet. Kenesta looked at Crista, who sat back in her spot and grabbed one piece. Kenesta imitated her and grabbed one piece herself.

The first bite was explosive. Never before had she experienced such an exquisite flavour. The flavours danced on the palate. They were like the rich and creamy essence of cheese. They had the vibrant, tangy notes of tomatoes and a subtle hint of spice. The dough was a masterpiece of culinary craft. It had been meticulously baked to perfection. Its golden outside yielded to reveal a tender and moist inside. From the moment Kenesta tasted the pizza, she fell in love with its flavours. The mere thought of that first bite left her yearning for more. An insatiable craving consumed her. Crista observed her from her vantage point, a smile gracing her lips as she nibbled on her own lower lip. With unwavering certainty, she possessed the knowledge that Kenesta would undoubtedly adore it.

Chapter 4

Kenesta sat in her bedroom. It used to be Crista's office, but she changed it just for her. Kenesta had been thinking about Crista too much in the last few days. She liked how Crista cared about her. She didn't expect it from a stranger. But with Crista, Kenesta felt like she was with an old friend or probably a lover. Since she was a child, she wanted her soulmate to be caring. Now she knew someone exactly like that, but she didn't know how to feel about it.

Crista was friendly, funny, and caring. She was patient with her. She tried hard to teach her English, and she never gave up, even if Kenesta made many mistakes. Kenesta sometimes wonders, though, if in this world, women dated women or if it was just men and women. She hoped not; she didn't like this stigma. She discovered it with a friend. Her friend was disgusted when they saw the same genre couple. Kenesta didn't understand why; it was absolutely natural. But this world would be different. It would be the opposite genre couple or the same genre couple. Or, it would be completely different, and no one dated here.

Kenesta wanted to ask Crista about this, but she was nervous. How was someone supposed to ask a question like this? Should she just come to Crista and ask her? Or should she ask her for a date and find out after that? The second option was more dangerous, and Kenesta didn't want to lose her new friendship with Crista. She had known her for just ten days, but Kenesta really appreciated their friendship.

During this week, Kenesta learned more about this world. She found the culture to be a little messed up with all the religions and different nations. There were even other holidays. Some of them sounded great, while others did not. However, Kenesta's love for food was profound. It consumed her. It was this love that truly captivated her. The delectable cuisine on offer was a feast for the senses. It was like the tasty flavours in a hot pizza. Also, she liked the savoury joy of Chinese noodles and liked the spices that defined Indian food. In her world, such things were conspicuously absent.

Kenesta also continued with her English lessons. She learned some basic phrases that she could use during her shopping trips. Also, Crista taught her to read and write in her alphabet, and it was funny. The symbols were different, but she liked them.

Throughout the week, she found herself gaining a new understanding of numbers. This was especially in relation to her shopping. It became clear that she needed to learn the numbers. She had to use them to find the amount she had to pay. However, Kenesta saw in this number an alternative purpose. It had a certain allure. She had a remarkable ability to see the precise amount of mystical energy needed. She deftly found the exact power needed to cast the spell. In the realm she inhabited, numerical values were not conveyed through conventional digits. Rather, they were expressed through the mystical language of runes.

"Kenesta, are you alright?" Crista asked her about their

telepathic bond. Crista went to the shop a few minutes earlier. She wanted to cook dinner for them, but they had an empty fridge.

"Yeah, I'm good. Did you buy everything?" Kenesta asked her. She loved their conversation when they didn't see each other.

"Yep, I will be home in a few minutes," Crista answered.

"Great."

The day before, Crista told Kenesta that she would be back to work in two weeks. Furthermore, she had told Kenesta that she would be left alone at home for the whole time. And so, they began the hard journey of honing their telepathic abilities. They worked to extend the range at which their minds could connect. Their purpose was clear: to set up a way to communicate across physical barriers. This would ensure their ability to stay connected, even in unexpected events.

Crista also thought about buying a phone for Kenesta. Still, it would be useless for her because she would not understand what Crista was telling her. But it should help with learning English. There were some useful apps for practising and learning. These apps served as a virtual sanctuary. They offered a place where people could immerse themselves in a world of interactive exercises and engaging lessons. All the content was carefully made to help people learn languages.

Crista came back from the shop and went to the kitchen. Kenesta joined her there, and together they started to prepare spaghetti Bolognese. Crista loved them, and Kenesta wanted to try them too. Crista found her mother's recipe, and together they began to prepare the ingredients.

"Would you like to watch a movie after dinner?" Crista asked Kenesta.

"If you would translate it," Kenesta said.

"Of course," Crista said with a smile.

Crista watched Kenesta's joy. She noticed changes in her after only a few days of living together. She was happier than she had been on her first day in the hospital. She was relaxed and asked more questions about this world. She even started showering every night.

The two young girls had a plate of steaming spaghetti. They gracefully made their way into the inviting living room. Crista was seated comfortably in her spot. She gracefully reached for the TV remote. Her delicate fingers deftly pressed its power button. With a flicker of light, the screen came to life, illuminating the room with its vibrant glow. A mischievous smile danced on Crista's lips. She navigated through the channels, searching for the perfect source of fun. Finally, her discerning gaze settled upon a comedy, a genre known to elicit laughter and mirth. She selected the programme with a gentle touch. It allowed the comedic story to unfold before their eager eyes. Watching was easy. The language was no problem. It allowed Kenesta to easily absorb more words.

"Can I ask you one question?" Crista asked while eating and watching comedy.

"Yes, of course."

"Did you have any boyfriends in your world?"

Kenesta looked at Crista in shock. What did she mean by this question?

"I—no, I didn't," Kenesta answered.

"Why not?"

"We don't date unless it is our soulmate."

"Oh," Crista said, shocked. "Did you have a crush on

someone?"

"I am not sure what that means."

"If you have some romantic feelings for someone."

"Umm, I guess." Kenesta looked at Crista; she didn't want to tell her that. "Did you love someone?"

"Yeah, there were a few girls I dated before," Crista replied, her gaze fixed on her plate.

"A girl?" Kenesta didn't know if her mind had translated it correctly. If it means that she should have a chance, Kenesta felt a flicker of hope ignite within her. Perhaps there was a possibility for a romantic connection with Crista after all.

"Yeah, I hope you don't mind it."

"No, of course not. I didn't know the dates' regulations in this world."

"I would not say regulation. It's more like prejudices on who you could date," Crista explained.

"Well, I don't know these prejudices, but we think you could be with anyone who liked you and didn't depend on their genre."

"That's better than here. Some people still don't like to see a homosexual couple, but it is better than it was just twenty years ago."

Crista found herself growing increasingly uneasy amidst the ongoing discourse. This prompted her to delicately propose a shift. She wanted to move from the current topic to something lighter.

ᕱᕱᕱ

Just 48 hours after the young women had an awkward exchange, Crista found herself browsing a platform for finding romance. She yearned to erase the last signs of her infatuation with Kenesta. She found herself yearning for a break from the tight grip of her emotions. In her room, Kenesta sat in deep thought. Her calm presence reminded her of the unreturned desires that plagued her. Crista held a deep fondness for her, cherishing the moments they spent together. But the bittersweet truth loomed over her. Kenesta's departure was imminent. It would leave Crista alone again.

Crista was swapping in the app when she got a notification about the match with another girl. Emotions swept through her. They were a mix of anticipation and trepidation. She found herself at a loss for words, unsure of what topics to broach with her. For a span of over six months, she abstained from the pursuit of romantic entanglements.

Hey, how are you? Crista wrote nervously. She hoped the other girl would respond.

Hi, not bad. Are you looking for something serious or just fun? Crista was confused when she read the answer from the girl. She didn't know what she was looking for.

I dunno, probably something serious; what about you? Crista was unsure of her answer. She wanted to just forget about her crush. She wasn't sure if it was going to be serious or just for fun.

I'm here mostly for fun, but we could try it. I haven't been in a serious relationship in a long time.

Me too.

Crista persisted in her writing for more than three hours. She did so alongside her companion. In the midst of her activities, she abruptly halted as Kenesta made her entrance into the room. With a swift motion, she reached out and got a tablet. She planned to improve her English using a children's app.

"What are you doing?" Kenesta asked her after a few hours of quiet between them.

"I am just writing to another girl."

"Oh, okay," Kenesta said, sounding sad, but it was probably just Crista's imagination.

Crista wanted to divert her thoughts. She resolved to press on with her writing. She would direct her attention to another young woman. This woman possessed a delightful sense of humour that matched her own. A twinge of guilt tugged at her heart as she contemplated the depth of her emotions for Kenesta. Yet, she knew deep down that she had to release her grip on these sentiments.

Kenesta just watched her with an unfamiliar feeling. The feeling that coursed through her was akin to a sharp blade piercing her very core. The concept eluded her comprehension. Her eyes were fixed on Crista, a subtle smile playing on her lips. The soft glow of her phone illuminated her face. She delicately tapped away, capturing her thoughts in written form. At this moment, a heavy feeling settled upon her. It made her seem more like a burden than the spirited person she once was.

With a heavy heart, Kenesta bid farewell to the familiar embrace of the living room. She yearned for the solace of her room. She found herself torn between the desire for solitude and the allure of a leisurely stroll. Longing for a breath of fresh air and a respite from the presence of Crista, she yearned to escape to a distant place. She followed a familiar path that led her to the park, a place she frequented often. She walked gracefully to one of the inviting benches. The benches lined the serene surroundings. Her gaze fell upon the tranquil river. Its gentle current flowed steadily. It seemed to whisper secrets to the world.

She thought about her new life. It was absolutely different. She missed her family and friends. She missed all the trips to the lake or the woods. She wanted to go back so badly, especially now. She hadn't expected to be so hurt when Crista told her about another girl, but she was.

Someone asked her, "Are you okay?"

Kenesta looked up. She was able to understand the words but didn't know how to respond. Crista told her to say something like 'fine' or 'good', but she didn't feel like that. She wasn't fine. Above her was a boy with brown skin. She never saw someone like him.

"I'm fine," she tried to say with the best pronunciation she could.

"You don't look like that. Are you sure that everything is alright?" She didn't seem to think she believed her. But she didn't understand the whole sentence she said, so she just nodded and hoped it would answer his question.

"I don't believe you," she didn't understand what he said; she only heard 'I' and 'don't', and the rest was lost to her.

"Sorry, I don't speak English," she said. Crista had taught her this sentence to use when she didn't understand something that someone said.

"Oh, sorry," he said and left Kenesta alone.

Most likely, just talking with a trusted friend would bring her comfort. However, her words remained unclear to those around her. She continued to struggle with the language barrier. She couldn't speak English fluently. In the vast expanse of solitude, she found herself in the company of her own thoughts. The absence of others enveloped her, casting a gentle shadow upon her existence.

Crista's worried voice asked, "Kenesta, where are you?"

Oh, she just found out; she is not home. Great. Did the girl stop speaking with her, and she decided to play again with Kenesta's feelings?

"Outside," she answered with anger.

"What happened?"

"Nothing." If she could, she would snarl.

"I can hear that something is not right, so what happened?"

"Nothing," Kenesta said, and she blocked their connection.

It was the first time in her life she found herself unwilling to engage in conversation with Crista. She yearned for solitude, a respite from the clamour of the world. Kenesta lingered outside, basking in the fading light of the day. She savoured the gentle caress of the cool evening breeze on her skin. The sun was slowly dipping below the horizon. It cast a mesmerising mix of colours across the sky. With each moment, the world around her changed, as shadows lengthened. She revelled in the ethereal dance of light. The sky changed from a delicate blue to a fiery red, before settling into a deep indigo. Unaware of the hour, she revelled in the simple pleasure of being outdoors.

When it was dark, she stood up and walked slowly to the exit from the park. On the way back home, she met Crista, who looked for her. She was worried, but Kenesta didn't speak with her. At home, Kenesta went straight to her room. She didn't want to speak with anyone, especially Crista. She looked at her worriedly, but Kenesta didn't care.

ᔕᔕᔕ

Crista was on her phone, writing to the girl whose name was Ellen. After three hours of writing, she was hungry. She made dinner for her and Kenesta, but she didn't answer when she called her name.

Crista went to her room and found it empty. She called her telepathically but got just one-word answers. And then she was unable to send other messages to her. It was like she hung up the phone and blocked the number. She was concerned for her. Crista left her for a few hours. If she was outside, she should be back before it gets dark.

But it was almost ten, and a cloak of darkness descended upon the world outside. Crista decided to go looking for her. She thought about where Kenesta could be, and just one place came to mind. It was a nearby park. Kenesta liked it and probably went there.

Crista went their usual way and hoped that she would meet her on the way, and she was lucky. Kenesta had just left the park when they met. But she didn't speak to her. At home, they went next to each other quietly. Crista didn't have any chance to talk with her. Their connection was still blocked.

At home, Kenesta went to her room before Crista could ask her about dinner. She could just watch her leave. It broke her heart, and she didn't know why. She had feelings for Kenesta, but she hadn't anticipated them being so strong. Now she didn't know what to do.

With a sense of urgency, Crista swiftly reached for her phone. Her fingers trembled slightly as she dialled a single, crucial number. In this desperate moment, she knew that only one person had the knowledge and expertise to aid her. Sabrina, a name that danced on the lips like a whisper in the wind. It carried the wind. She fervently hoped that sleep had not yet claimed her.

After three rings, Sabrina picked up the phone.

"Hello?" She sounded confused.

"Hi, I think I need your help," Crista said without waiting.

"Crista! What happened to you? The boss told me you have some family emergencies. Is everything alright?"

"No, I think I fucked up. Can we meet tomorrow? I need to speak to someone."

"Yes, of course, I have a night shift, so we can meet at ten in Boston Tea if it's alright?"

"Yes, thank you."

"No problem; see you tomorrow, and please try to get some sleep before. Don't worry, we manage it together."

"Thanks, good night."

Crista hung up the phone and went to the bathroom. She couldn't sleep. So, she took solace in a steamy shower. She hoped it would calm the restlessness in her. The waterfall offered a brief rest. Its rhythmic pattern was a lullaby for her troubled mind. Eventually, Crista reluctantly retreated to her bed. The allure of sleep overshadowed her insatiable curiosity. She succumbed to temptation. She reached for her phone and unlocked its digital realm with a flicker of excitement. Her heart skipped a beat. She anxiously scanned the dating app, her eyes searching for a message from Ellen. She had written to her an hour before and was worried when she didn't answer.

Sorry, my housemate was lost, and I had to find her; she is new here. Crista wrote to her. She still felt guilty about writing to a stranger, but Sabrina would help her tomorrow.

That's fine. I hope they are okay. Do you want to meet next week?

I don't know. We just met; should we wait a little longer?

Yes, of course. I have to go to sleep; I have work tomorrow. Good night, X.

Good night.

Crista tried to fall asleep, but it didn't help. She wanted to know what happened to Kenesta since she didn't speak with her. She lay in her bed for two hours until sleep came, but it wasn't a restful one.

ᏅᏅᏅ

The following day, Crista woke up around six. She had strange dreams about the magic world and speaking animals. Yet, they did not comfort her. They only made her more worried about Kenesta. Her heart was heavy with concern. She yearned for the coming hours to reveal the answers she sought.

Crista went to the kitchen because she needed coffee and something to eat. She also prepared breakfast for Kenesta. She didn't know when she would wake up, but she knew that Kenesta would be hungry because she had missed dinner.

Crista sat in the kitchen with her phone and drank her coffee. She stayed there in the hope of meeting Kenesta and finally speaking about the previous day. But Kenesta didn't come until Crista had to leave for a meeting with Sabrina.

Crista was disappointed and hoped Kenesta would be there when she returned.

Crista walked quickly to the coffee shop. She liked the coffee there; it was one of the best coffee places in Worcester. Sabrina wasn't there yet, so Crista chose a table downstairs, so Sabrina could see her when she came. Meanwhile, she ordered a large salad and ham and cheese toast. She had eaten a few hours earlier and was hungry again.

Sabrina went to the coffee place a few minutes after ten. It was at that exact moment that Crista got her toast.

"Hey," Sabrina said as she approached her. But first, she stopped by a court to order coffee and show the barrister where she could bring it. "How are you?"

"Not good. What about you?" Crista wanted to start with small talk before they started talking about her problem.

"Busy because someone doesn't work," Sabrina said with a smirk.

"I'm sorry, but I have a good reason."

"Really?" Sabrina raised one of her eyebrows.

"Yeah, do you remember the girl?" Crista waited until Sabrina nodded and said, "Well, she lives with me now. I am helping her learn English." She started off and told her everything about Kenesta.

Sabrina was listening patiently. She had some questions but waited until Crista finished her explanation. Meanwhile, she sipped her coffee, which had been brought to her by the waitress.

Crista concluded her speech by saying, "And now she doesn't speak with me."

"Well, it really seems like you fucked up," Sabrina said. She was confused about why Crista had allowed this mess into her life. She tried to recapitulate everything. Crista asked her a question about the situation. She wanted to know why she thinks this happened or how she feels about Kenesta. They did not, however, leave the situation.

"I think you could try to meet with Ellen. She sounds like a good girl to me. You also have to distance yourself from the Kenesta. Otherwise, you will be miserable," Sabrina said after a long pause.

"How could I possibly do it?"

"You should probably get back to work. You would be away and should find that the feeling isn't real."

"All right, I'll call Jeremy and see if he can get me some shifts," Crista agreed with her.

"Great, I would have to go. I need to prepare some stuff before work but remember, call Jeremy today and leave Kenesta alone. It would help both of you."

Sabrina left the coffee place. They had been talking for over an hour. It was time for her to go home and make some food. She had a night shift in the restaurant. Crista watched her leave and decided to call her boss immediately. Sabrina had a point. They were probably too long together, and some time alone would help them.

"Hello, Crista," her boss said as she answered the phone.

"Hi, I just want to tell you that I changed my mind and want to go back to work."

"Great, I can write to you next week if it works for you."

"Yes, that would be great; thank you."

"I thank you. I will send you your shifts when they are ready."

"Yes, perfect. See you."

"See you."

After the call, Crista chose to go out and explore the shops that lined the bustling streets. She aimed to buy something for her own pleasure. She yearned for a fresh experience, a departure from the familiar.

Kenesta woke up around nine, but she didn't want to leave her warm bed. So, she lay there and grabbed one of the workbooks. She worked on her reading and writing skills until she heard the front door shut. That had to mean that Crista went outside. She probably went on a date with the girl she wrote to yesterday.

Kenesta couldn't help but feel a pang of jealousy towards the girl. In the depths of her heart, she harboured a profound affection for Crista. She yearned for Crista's presence to be exclusively hers. The notion did not sit well with her. Inevitably, she found herself facing the prospect of sharing her space. However, amid the chaos and uncertainty in this world, this thing stood out. It was the sole beacon of truth and righteousness. She would leave gracefully and say goodbye. Crista, steadfast and resolute, would stay here.

Kenesta went to the kitchen to find an empty room with a plate on the table. She didn't expect Crista to cook breakfast for her, but this made her day. She was literally starving, and the food looked so good.

Kenesta ate all the food and moved to the living room. She switched on the TV and put some children's cartoons on. It was easy to understand, and Kenesta found herself enjoying these things. Crista didn't come home for another three hours, and Kenesta didn't mind it. She didn't know what she would tell her. She was angry, but she was also sorry. She was embarrassed about her outburst.

Kenesta had no right to be consumed by jealousy. She was jealous of her writing to another girl. She did not possess her, nor was she, her companion. After much thought, Kenesta realised her initial view was flawed. However, the notion of offering an apology did not resonate with her. Instead of dwelling on an apology, Kenesta chose to focus on a tangible gesture of goodwill. With purpose, she set about preparing a tasty lunch. It would feed and connect them.

Kenesta had to wait for Crista until two o'clock in the afternoon. However, the anticipation proved to be worthwhile. Crista arrived home, her stomach growling with hunger, burdened by an array of bags. She saw the tasty spread on the table. A strong desire surged within her. It compelled her to fling herself into Kenesta's arms. She longed to hug her passionately. However, she refrained from committing the act.

For the remainder of the day, the girls found solace in the comforting glow of the television screen. Their words hung in the air as if caught in a delicate dance of silence.

Chapter 5

Two weeks had passed since Crista had returned to work. From the outset, a formidable challenge presented itself to both young girls. Crista's worry for Kenesta weighed on her mind. It caused her to reach out to her at every chance during her workday. She yearned for reassurance. She sought solace in knowing her dear friend was safe. Kenesta, however, found herself engulfed in boredom. She was in the confines of her humble abode.

The first few days, she tried to work on her English and vocabulary. Still, after five days, she didn't have enough motivation to continue. She tried everything, but her English did not improve, so she gave up. She stopped watching TV. Without Crista, it wasn't the same and wasn't interesting anymore.

Crista remained silent, her lips sealed in a tight line, for a time was a luxury she simply couldn't afford. She diligently occupied her time at work, faithfully attending almost every day. She was rarely given a break. But, when she was, they would go on trips to shop. She texted Ellen. After much thought, they agreed to meet on a day when Crista was free of work. Today was the day that had been eagerly anticipated.

Crista's heart fluttered with anticipation as she prepared to meet Ellen. The idea of meeting the famous person filled her with excitement. The air crackled with electric energy. Crista's mind raced with the possibilities of their encounter. For over two weeks, their conversations flowed effortlessly. They were like a symphony of words and shared understanding. Crista harboured a glimmer of hope. She yearned to be the chosen one, desperate to erase the memory of her infatuation with Kenesta. Crista carefully selected her best dress. She considered the pleasant warmth outside. She was looking forward to the upcoming meeting at the grand cathedral. She wanted to present herself in the most elegant and captivating way. The bustling locale was full of activity. It offered many charming cafés and exquisite restaurants. They were for those seeking a delicious dining experience.

Kenesta watched Crista preparing for the date, a pang of sorrow tugging at her heart. In her heart, she harboured a fervent hope. She hoped their paths would never cross. From this day on, their lives would remain separate and far. However, those aspirations were merely figments of her imagination. She was certain. The young girl would surely grow fond of Crista. Crista had a gentle and compassionate nature. She had an innate ability to inspire affection and admiration in all who crossed her path. Her true kindness and love for others made it almost inconceivable for anyone to feel any animosity towards her.

"I am going; I will be home before night," Crista said before leaving.

"Enjoy," Kenesta said without emotion. She didn't want to show how hurt she was.

Crista gave her a gentle smile and said goodbye. She gracefully left the flat, waving her hand in a small, elegant gesture. Kenesta's gaze lingered on the door as it softly shut, sealing off the outside world. With a sigh, she turned away, her thoughts drifting back to the sanctuary of her room. To find out if her magical core had matured, she meditated briefly. However, the past few weeks have yielded only minimal advancements. Despite her best efforts, she still lacked the power to conjure any spells. Each attempt left her utterly depleted, drained to the very depths of her being.

Kenesta awoke from her meditation and jotted down her thoughts in her notebook. She kept this one in a secret space behind her bed. She didn't want Crista to see it. There were some of her drawings of Crista's face, as well as some of her thoughts. It was written in her mother tongue, but she still didn't feel comfortable showing it to someone.

After an hour, Kenesta decided to go on a walk. She was already bored at home, and she wanted fresh air after today. And she could practice her spoken English, even if she could not speak it fluently.

Kenesta strolled along her beloved path towards the bustling heart of the city. With her, she carried a sum of money bestowed upon her by Crista. Crista bestowed it upon her, a token of potential indulgence. Should she desire to procure something of her choosing? On this day, she felt compelled to enter a welcoming local coffee shop. Crista had already shared her wisdom. She had guided her on the art of ordering at the restaurant she longed to try.

It was sunny outside, and the city centre was bustling with shoppers. Kenesta liked to watch people walking along the street, and she was one of them now. She went inside one cafeteria and ordered a caramel latte. She didn't know what it meant, but the woman before she ordered it too, and it sounded good. The air in the shop smelled delicious.

The cashier asked her if she wanted it inside or out. Kenesta decided to sit down and enjoy her coffee. The cashier smiled at her accent but didn't say anything. They would happily serve people from different countries. As Crista said, British people were used to it.

Kenesta waited for her order. Then, she chose a table near the windows to watch people outside. Only moments had passed since her arrival. Her gaze fell upon Crista, who stood with an unfamiliar young lady. They engaged in lively conversation, their laughter filling the air. Kenesta's fragile hopes for Crista's affection were mercilessly shattered. It was like a wooden boat succumbing to jagged rocks.

The girl possessed an undeniable allure, her beauty radiating from every angle. Yet, there was something more to her than mere physicality. A glimmer in her eyes hinted at a playful spirit. It suggested that she had a delightful sense of humour. Crista's laughter filled the air, her joyous peals echoing through the room. With each burst of mirth, she couldn't help but draw attention to her graceful neck, a sight to behold. Crista longed for a companion like her, who had her qualities. They would bring her joy and peace. Kenesta hailed from a distant celestial realm. The spoken language there bore no resemblance to earthly tongues. As a result, Kenesta communicated only with enigmatic telepathic transmissions. They went beyond normal speech. Kenesta was overcome by a profound sense of darkness that seemed to envelop her very being. Also, a young girl approached her table. She politely asked if she might join her.

"Is everything alright?" Someone asked Kenesta.

Kenesta looked up and saw a blonde girl with glasses smiling at her.

"I… I… no," she said after a long time of thinking.

"You look like you have had a shock. Do you need someone to talk to?" The girl tried. Kenesta didn't know her, but she needed someone to share her feelings with. Perhaps a stranger might be the perfect person.

"I don't speak English well. I worried," Kenesta explained.

"It doesn't matter. I am not a native either. Just try to express yourself with the words you know," the girl said with a smile. Kenesta was surprised; her English sounded great. How is it possible?

"I like one girl, but… she," Kenesta was at a loss for words.

"You don't know if she wants you back," the girl suggested.

Kenesta shook her head. "She is concerned, but she… and girl…" Kenesta tried to say what she wanted, but it was challenging and frustrating.

"She is with another girl," the girl tried to guess.

Kenesta nodded.

"Are you housemates?" The girl asked, but Kenesta didn't know this word and looked confused.

"Do you live together?" The girl tried a little differently.

"Yes, she teach English I," Kenesta said.

"That's good," the girl smiled, "and by the way, I am Pavlina, but you can call me Pav."

Kenesta smiled at her name; it was beautiful, and the conversation with Pav was easy.

They spent another hour or so just speaking. Kenesta really enjoyed talking with someone who didn't speak English as their mother tongue.

"Would you like to meet again tomorrow, so we can practise your English together? You could bring your books," Pav asked. And Kenesta agreed with her. It should be fun to have someone else to practice with. They wouldn't judge her because they know the struggles of English.

Pavlina had to leave because she had a meeting with one of her friends. But they agreed to meet at the same coffee place the next day at ten o'clock. They'd have enough time to practise their English. Pav was confident that this would help Kenesta more than her practice with Crista. Kenesta did not rush home as soon as her obligations were fulfilled. Instead, she decided to leisurely peruse the shops that lined the bustling streets. She let herself fully immerse herself in the vibrant atmosphere. She silently prayed with fear. She prayed that fate would not bring her path together with Crista and the enigmatic girl again.

Crista enjoyed her day with Ellen. The date was a success. Ellen had a delightful sense of humour. She effortlessly wove laughter into every interaction. Her kindness radiated from within. It touched the lives of all lucky enough to cross her path. However, Kenesta did not share the sentiments that enveloped Crista. Ellen was pleasant, but something was missing in their interactions. In Kenesta's presence, an ineffable charm existed. It happened whenever they went outside or stayed at home.

Kenesta just shone with positivity, and the room looked more alive. It was like magic. Crista said this because Kenesta is not from a magical realm, as one might assume. Ellen possessed an undeniable charm, captivating Crista's heart with every glance. She embodied everything Crista had yearned for in a partner. She was a perfect example of her ideal girlfriend. However, it was not Kenesta.

After this day, Crista knew that her feelings for Kenesta weren't just a crush. Suddenly, she understood that she loved Kenesta. She decided to find a way for the two girls to be together. Crista knew that with Kenesta, her life was whole.

After four hours spent with Ellen, Crista went home; she was full of doubts about her decision to go on this date. She enjoyed her time, but she missed Kenesta. No effort was made on her part to reach out, leaving her consumed by a sense of guilt. What if fate, in its capricious nature, were to cast its shadow upon her? Crista hurried home, her steps quick and purposeful. She entered her familiar abode. Her eyes were drawn to Kenesta. She was seated gracefully on the sofa. A book, its pages filled with the intricacies of the English language, lay open in her hands.

"Hi, how your date?" Kenesta looked up at her.

Crista was shocked when she heard her speak English. She made a mistake, but she sounds more confident.

"Well, it was good, but I was missing something," Crista said simply. She didn't know how far Kenesta was from her understanding, and she felt worse than before. She neglected Kenesta just because she was scared of her. This had to change.

"Good," Kenesta said as she resumed reading.

"How was your day?" Crista really felt terrible for neglecting this amazing creature. Crista wanted to get back to their feelings when they first got together. This was in the weeks after the hospital when all they did was spend time with each other.

"Good, I was outside and met a girl named Pav; she offered to practice with me her English. She from some country in Czechia or something. But she know the struggle with teach language," Kenesta answered excitedly. Her English was better.

"That sounds great," Crista said, smiling at her but feeling a stab in her heart.

"Of course, we meet tomorrow."

"Good. Did you eat?" Crista changed the conversation.

"Yes, there is also one for you."

Crista nodded and went to the kitchen to see what Kenesta had prepared for them. It looked terrific, but she didn't know what it was. She tried a bit, and it tasted as good as it looked. Kenesta really knew how to cook.

When Crista finished her food, she moved into the living room, where she sat on the other sofa and switched on the TV.

"Do you want to watch a movie?" She asked Kenesta.

"Sure, could we watch some comedy with subtitles, please?"

"Of course," Crista replied, selecting one of her favourite films, Love, Simon. She turned on the subtitles for Kenesta. She then enjoyed the rest of the day with Kenesta watching TV. But both women were thinking about how they wanted each other. But they couldn't find the words to say it. The tension simmered like a heat wave.

The next day, Crista left around nine o'clock because she had to go to work. Kenesta, for the first time, didn't mind it. She was excited to meet her new friend and practice her English with someone other than Crista. Kenesta wore one of her dresses. She loved dresses. It was light. On top of it, she wore one of the leather jackets Crista bought her the first week.

She went to the same cafeteria as the day before. She also ordered the same coffee. It was delicious, and she wanted it again. The coffee place was busier than the day before, but she still managed to find a seat near the windows.

Pav arrived fashionably late, a touch of nonchalance in his stride. Yet, Kenesta, ever the gracious hostess, paid no mind to his tardiness. She was engrossed in one of her books. She delved into the depths of knowledge, eagerly learning new words with each turn of the page. The room was filled with lively chatter and animated discussions. It had a refreshing ambience. It was a change from the solitude of her study. Here, amidst the vibrant atmosphere, she found joy in honing her linguistic skills. She effortlessly learned the details of the language. She did it by immersing herself in the ebb and flow of nearby conversations.

"Hi, how are you?" Pav walked to her table with her own coffee.

"Hi, good, how you?" Kenesta really enjoyed the way Pav spoke. It wasn't as fast as Crista, and she made sure Kenesta understood her.

"Good, good. Did you speak with your friend yesterday?"

"Yes, we watch TV yesterday. She work today."

Pav smiled at her simple sentences. It was cute.

"That is your book?"

Kenesta nodded and gave it to Pav. She looked into it.

"I used some when I learned English in school. These are good for you."

Kenesta smiled at her, and they started to work on some exercises in the books. Kenesta enjoyed it because Pav gave her a new view of learning. Crista wasn't a lousy teacher, but she didn't know the struggle of learning and speaking a foreign language.

The day spent in the company of Pav proved to be nothing short of extraordinary. Her humour was undeniable. It effortlessly wove into her explanations of grammar and word use. After two hours, Kenesta found herself enriched with many new words. She also gained a basic grasp of grammar. They stood in the coffee shop for the whole time and ordered some food when it was lunchtime.

But Pav had to leave after midday. She had lectured at the university. Kenesta didn't know what it was, and Pav decided to show her one of the buildings. Kenesta's heart fluttered with anticipation. She eagerly awaited the sight of something new. They strolled together, their steps in perfect harmony. Pav unveiled a new path. It was a route that led to a place where she would ultimately reside alongside Crista.

Pav showed her the library. They decided to meet there the next day because they could use other books. Moreover, the library boasted an additional coffee establishment. It would undoubtedly serve as a delightful respite during their collaborative sessions.

All in all, Kenesta enjoyed these lessons. And she decided to ask Crista about the phone and the social media Pav was talking about. It would be great for her to talk with her new friend from home. She could also practice her written English.

For the rest of the day, Kenesta stayed home. She finally found learning English fun and wanted to learn more and faster. They agreed with Pav that Kenesta would learn another chapter and they would go over it the next day. Pav would explain something, but Kenesta didn't understand.

Around two o'clock, Crista contacted her to ask how she was doing and about her lessons with Pav. Kenesta was glad to describe all she learned that day. Crista had to stop her with laughter. Crista was happy for her, but she wanted to hear everything when she would be home, which would be after five o'clock.

Kenesta agreed to not say more. She was looking forward to telling her about Pav, their coffee time, the walk, and more. And for the first time, she had to say it in English, so Kenesta was happy to wait.

The evening came fast, and Crista finally arrived home from work. Kenesta was excited and prepared for them some of her mother's food. Cooking was hard because she lacked the right ingredients. But, she managed to make it taste the same as she remembered from her home.

This brought her to think of what her family did, and if they missed her the same way she did she missed them.

Crista was anxious at work. She worried about Kenesta and leaving her with a foreign girl she hadn't met yet. Also, Sabrina was asking about her date. She told her everything. Sabrina advised her to talk about her feelings with Kenesta. They probably found a solution together.

Crista decided to do it this evening. She wanted to know where she was with Kenesta and probably work on it. On the way home, she stopped in a shop and bought a bottle of red wine and roses for Kenesta. She didn't know their dating stories, but she wanted to do it right. And she hoped Kenesta would love the roses.

Crista came to her flat and found Kenesta already sitting in the kitchen and eating her dinner. Crista looked at her and decided to wait until after dinner. She brought the roses to her room and took the wine to the kitchen.

"I thought we could have a nice evening. I bought wine for us," Crista told Kenesta.

"Good, I prepare food. I hope you will like it."

"Of course, I already love your cooking," Crista said, and she started eating her dinner. As she suspected, it was delicious, as was every meal Kenesta cooked.

After dinner, they moved to the living room. But before that, Crista poured wine into two glasses and brought them. And then she jumped to her room and grabbed the roses and went back to the living room.

"Kenesta," she started nervously, "I know we've only known each other a few weeks. But I found out during that time that I have feelings for you. I want to ask; will you be my girlfriend?"

With the last word, Crista gave the roses to Kenesta, who was in shock. She didn't expect it, especially after the day before, when Crista was on a date with another girl. Kenesta watched Crista and didn't know what to say. Should she agree? Should she dismiss her? Or was it just a joke and she was supposed to laugh? She was lost.

"Please say something," Crista was scared when Kenesta didn't say anything. It should mean she didn't like her or that she hates her now.

Kenesta was sitting on the sofa without moving. She didn't know. She felt the same, but she didn't want to disappoint Crista. What if Crista wasn't her soulmate? But what if she was and she admitted it? She had to consider it.

"I understand," Crista said sadly after a few minutes of silence. She put the roses on the table and left the room. Kenesta watched her leave and decided.

"Wait," she said.

Crista turned around with hope on her face.

"I would love to be your girlfriend; I just don't want to disappoint you because I don't know exactly what this means."

"Thanks!" Crista said loudly and ran to hug Kenesta. She was happy and didn't even think that Kenesta would disappoint her.

"So, what does it mean? We are partners now?" Kenesta asked.

"That means we have to go on dates, lots of dates," Crista said, not stopping to smile. She was happy and was looking for their future.

"Like you were yesterday with the girl?"

"Yes, but this would be much better than with her. I will bring you to the fair. We will go on a trip around the UK. We could also go abroad if you would like," Crista said.

"It sounds good, but I think we need to take it slow. We have known each other for just four weeks." Kenesta laughed at her excitement.

"Of course, but this will be amazing, I promise."

With a smile gracing her lips, Kenesta made the conscious choice to take another step forward. Her heart yearned for the touch of Crista's lips upon her own. She inched closer to her slowly and carefully. Her intentions were veiled in secrecy. Then, in a moment that caught Crista completely off guard, she pressed her lips against hers. It was a surprising and unforeseen act of intimacy. She proceeded without protest.

She expounded on her thoughts and had an intricate chat with Kenesta. Kenesta's heart fluttered with excitement. She leaned in and her lips gently met Crista's. It was a moment of pure innocence and vulnerability. It was a first kiss that held the promise of something beautiful. In that fleeting instant, Kenesta felt overwhelming gratitude. Fate had chosen Crista to share this milestone with her.

Chapter 6

When Kenesta met with Pav the next day, she was in a much better mood and couldn't wait until she told her new friend. Crista went with her because she wanted to know who this girl was and if she was safe for Kenesta. She didn't trust strangers who just came and helped other people. She suspected that her actions were motivated by evil intentions.

Kenesta and Crista came to the library and waited in front of the building. They held hands, and Kenesta really enjoyed this small stuff. She wanted to show that Crista is her and they are together.

Pav arrived a little late, like the last day, but it was just two minutes, and even she wasn't alone. She came along with another girl. They both spoke a new language, and Kenesta was surprised to hear a new language. She was aware that there existed additional languages. Yet, what she heard bore no resemblance to English. In Olostia, the language was a little similar, but this was a new kind of language.

"Oh, hi, sorry I am late. Alice wanted to go with me. She studies English. She has a course for teaching English as a second language," Pav said, looking at Crista.

"Don't worry," Kenesta assured her, "this Crista, my…" Her voice trailed off as she struggled to find the right term to describe their relationship.

"Her girlfriend," Crista finished without feeling ashamed.

"Nice to meet you. Kenesta was talking a lot about you," Pav said with a smile.

Crista said coldly, "Hope, only in good."

"Of course. Would you join us today?" Pav asked, her voice laced with curiosity. To Crista's surprise, she was unfazed by the question. Her manner was calm and composed.

"No, I have to work today, but I wanted to see who Kenesta was meeting with."

"That is understandable, but don't worry, we won't hurt her."

"Ok, I have to go," Crista said and turned to Kenesta, "See you in the evening."

Before she left, she kissed Kenesta.

"I want details," Pav said after Crista disappeared on the way to the city centre.

"There's none," Kenesta said with a blush. She wasn't used to this, but she loved it.

"Oh, come on, how did that happen? Who took the first step? How did you meet?" Pav talked too fast, and Kenesta had a problem catching all the questions.

"Paya, slow down," Alice said for the first time. She had a really melodic voice, similar to one of Kenesta's friends.

"But…" Pav wanted to argue.

"Ne, je ne, dostaneš svoje detaily, but not today.[8]" Alice switched between two languages so easily that she probably didn't know it.

"What language do you speak?" Kenesta was curious. It sounded different from English.

"Czech, we are both from the same country," Alice told her.

"But how do you talk two languages at once?"

"It's called code-switching. You would do it too when you spoke English better," Alice explained.

"Can assist me?" Kenesta asked. She didn't know she used the wrong sentence structure, but both girls understood her.

"We will try our best to help you," Pav said.

"Can we go inside? We should speak more when we sit down," Alice suggested.

"Indeed," both young ladies agreed. Their eyes were bright with anticipation. They were climbing the grand staircase to the library's third floor. They made their way to a cosy nook with a graceful stride. The nook was near the towering windows that filled the room with a soft, ethereal glow.

Alice took out some books from her backpack. The books looked small and not heavy. But their weight should increase. There were six books about learning a second language and English grammar.

"I used these books to learn English. They could help you with most of the practical parts of the language," Alice said. She pointed at two books about English grammar. "And my lecturer recommended these books."

"Where can we start?" Pav clapped her hands in excitement. Kenesta didn't share her enthusiasm but was willing to learn English for Crista.

"I would suggest starting with sentence structure," Alice said. Pav and Kenesta agreed. They spent around two hours explaining the importance of sentence structure. They also explained how to use it in different types of sentences. Kenesta was exhausted after it. She didn't see any reason to learn about this or why to use it.

But Alice and Pav had patience with her and explained it again and again until she understood it. Alice also recommended reading English books. They would help her build her vocabulary. They said that doing so would make her grammar more natural. Kenesta wasn't against that idea, as she loved reading in her dimension.

After two hours, they took a break from learning and just talked. Kenesta asked both girls about the other language they spoke. She asked about their experience with learning English. Both girls had different learning experiences. Kenesta was amazed that they both spoke so well. However, she did not hear their errors as someone who spoke English as their first language would.

After another hour of just talking, they decided to end their session and go home, as Pav and Alice had other plans. Kenesta agreed with them, told them goodbye, and went back. She came in the morning with Crista. Alice and Pav kept an eye on her until she vanished around the bend.

"So, what do you think about her?" Pav asked on the way home.

"Well, she is interesting, but do you know where she is from?"

"No, her accent is hard to read, and she didn't say."

"Exactly, it is weird. Probably we should ask her next time."

"Agree."

Kenesta hurried home, her heart brimming with anticipation. She was excited to share her new knowledge and progress in English with Crista. She was delighted by the exchange. She had shared it with the young women. It made her heart swell with affection. Their friendly nature had left an indelible impression. It made her consider confiding in them and baring her soul with honesty. However, she wanted to consult Crista first. She knew that Crista might not be content. However, a sense of assurance washed over her as she contemplated the young women before her. Despite their short acquaintance, she was sure of their honesty and trustworthiness.

The realisation swept through her being, akin to a gust of fresh air filling her lungs. In the vast unfamiliar realm, she found a group of trustworthy people. This lucky meeting with kindred souls brought much joy. It filled her with contentment, spreading through her. In her small home, she had made friends with many different species. However, in this new place, her social circle had shrunk to include only Crista. Perhaps now, she'll add Pav and Alice. And she adored it. She loved being with many people. She found joy in their presence. And she loved it. She loved to have many people around her. She could have fun with people or creatures, run around the forest, and do other things. And now that she has the language, she will be able to have more friends.

In a good mood, she arrived at the empty flat; Crista was still at work. Most likely, she would be there until late at night. Kenesta didn't mind being alone, but she wanted to share her knowledge from today with someone. She needed someone to speak with, and in the empty flat, she was unable. But first, she needed something to eat.

She began preparing some food while humming a melody she had probably heard in the city centre. After a couple of minutes, she put some music on and made it a happier place for her. With music playing, the flat didn't seem to be empty anymore.

After an hour, Kenesta started to feel lonely. She read a book to grow her vocabulary. But the empty flat didn't help her to concentrate. So she decided to visit Crista at work and show her how she improved her speaking. As she decided, she put some dresses on, grabbed a handbag, and went.

The restaurant where Crista worked wasn't too far away. It was around five minutes' walk. And with Kenesta's determination, she was there in four.

The restaurant wasn't busy. A couple of tables were occupied by customers with pints of beer. Some of them also had food. But it was mostly quiet there. Crista was nowhere to be seen. But it was alright; she was probably in the kitchen with food orders or in the basement for drinks, and they ran out.

Kenesta went straight to the bar. One of Crista's colleagues was serving another customer. While she was waiting, she picked what she would like to drink. She didn't want anything alcoholic as she wanted to continue her studies, but lemonade or tea would be nice.

When it was her turn to order, she said, "Hi, could I order raspberry lemonade?"

"Sure, it would be £2.50—card or cash?" The girl behind the bar asked her.

"Er, card, please."

"Just tap here. The drink will be ready in a minute," the girl said. She motioned to the machine on the bar and began making Kenesta drinks. Kenesta held her card above the device until it made a peep sound, and that put the card back into the purse.

"Perfect. Everything is alright. Here is your drink," said the girl. She turned back with the drink and checked the device to see if Kenesta had paid.

With a graceful gesture, Kenesta delicately grasped the glass. Its cool surface sent a shiver of excitement up her arm. She made her way to the beer garden. It was a hidden oasis in the bustling city, offering a break from urban chaos. As she arrived, a breathtaking view appeared before her. The tranquil canal stretched out like a liquid ribbon. It reflected the golden hues of the setting sun. Only three more customers remained in the establishment. Kenesta carefully selected a table. It was near the tranquil canal. She gracefully sat in the seat. With a graceful motion, she retrieved her cherished book from its resting place. She was eager to immerse herself in its captivating pages again. She resumed reading, letting the words transport her to another world. Particularly so, given her lack of knowledge regarding Crista's current whereabouts.

After some time, Crista came out to check on customers in the beer garden. She looked to see if anyone needed anything or if there were any empty glasses to collect. It was also at this time that she saw Kenesta sitting by one of the tables and reading. At one moment, she was surprised to see her.

She went to her and said, "Hi, what are you doing here?"

Kenesta looked up from her book and smiled at her: "Hi, I'm bored, so go visit me."

Kenesta put lots of effort into the words; she wasn't sure about grammar, but she just felt the way she spoke was correct.

"That's good to hear. How were your study lessons?" Crista smiled at her bad sentence structure but didn't say anything. She liked the way Kenesta was speaking.

"Good, I learned something new… hm…" Kenesta was looking for vocabulary, "item?"

"You mean new things?" Crista laughs at her choice, but she understands it.

"Yes, that thing!" Kenesta was happy. She didn't mind Crista laughing, as she knew she didn't mean it to be taken that way.

"That's good. Will you wait here until I finish?" Crista asked, and Kenesta just nodded. Crista went back to her duties, and Kenesta went back to reading.

Crista was working all the time. When she went to the garden, she looked after Kenesta to see if she needed anything. Fortunately, Kenesta was just sitting by her table, reading. Crista was scared that Kenesta could disappear from the seat. After all, this is where Kenesta appeared a couple of weeks ago. Crista wasn't comfortable with Kenesta being here.

But, so far, everything has gone well until one moment when Crista went to check the garden one more time. Kenesta wasn't behind her table. There was only her book, and half of her drank the drink. Crista panicked, then calmed down. She should only be on the toilet; there's no need to panic over it.

Crista left the garden, intending to return in a few minutes to make sure Kenesta hadn't vanished.

Kenesta went to the bathroom. Her hands were sticky. She didn't like to touch her book with dirty hands. When she came out of the bathroom, she saw a nice mirror on the wall. The frame was similar to one she saw in the shop at her home. She touched the edge because she liked the structure and wanted to feel it.

As her fingertips grazed the frame, gentle warmth enveloped her. It was as if enchantment itself lived within. Curiosity flickered within her. It prompted her to ask Crista about the mirror's origins. Perhaps, she pondered, Crista held the key to unlocking its secrets. With this in mind, she decided to retreat to her table. She would patiently wait until Crista's shift ended. It was then, she surmised, that she would seize the opportunity to pose her inquiries. Could this be the elusive pathway leading her back to her own realm? Only time would reveal the truth.

Crista finished within an hour. During that time, she checked Kenesta a couple of times. She did so, especially after she got back from the toilet. She was terrified. She vanished when she didn't want to, not just to the toilet, but permanently from her life.

When Crista finished her shift, she went straight to the Kenesta table and hugged her as hard as she could. For now, Kenesta was still with her. Kenesta was gobsmacked by the hug, but she returned it. She felt safe in Crista's arms, so she didn't mind.

"Can I ask you something?" Kenesta used their telepathic connection.

"Yeah, sure, what is it?" Crista nodded and looked at her without breaking the hug.

"I saw a mirror when I was on the toilet, and I want to know if you can tell me something about it."

"Which mirror do you mean?" Crista tried to keep calm, but the question surprised her, and she hoped that Kenesta didn't mean the one she felt.

"The one with the decorative frame. It appears to be from my world," Kenesta clarified.

Crista couldn't think of anything to say. She tightened her grip as if she were scared. Kenesta disappeared at that moment.

"Is everything alright?" Kenesta asked after a couple of seconds when Crista didn't say anything.

"Yeah, I don't want to speak about that," Crista said aloud, "let's go home." She let Kenesta go of her arms and grabbed her bag so they could leave as soon as possible.

"All right," Kenesta said, unsure what it meant. She took her stuff, and together they left. But as they were walking, they passed the mirror, and Kenesta stopped. Something was different about the image she saw inside.

Kenesta turned her gaze to Crista and saw the worry in her eyes. She looked scared and was shaking. Kenesta looked in the mirror again. Then she turned away, her focus now fixed solely on Crista, as a decision formed in her mind. At this critical juncture, Crista's well-being took precedence over all else. She held her friends' safety dear. But she could set it aside for now. Crista stood before Kenesta and needed her help. Kenesta's unwavering devotion now fell on Crista.

"Please don't touch it," she heard after she decided; it was just like a whisper, but she could feel the urge of the world.

"I won't, don't worry," she said when she touched Crista's face and kissed her on the forehead. "I would never leave you alone."

Crista nodded, not trusting her voice. Kenesta held her hand and led them to the street, where they continued on their way home. The girls were holding hands to reassure each other. They were saying that nothing happened and that they were still together.

The way was quick and quiet. None of the girls wanted to speak about the mirror or what should happen if Kenesta touched it. Crista was still shaking. She imagined that she would lose Kenesta. Kenesta thought about her friends and family she saw in the mirror. They were looking for someone.

They walked quietly. They met people who were watching them. Some looked with disgust, and some were supportive. But none of them stopped them and talked to them. They were just watching them from afar.

"Do you want to grab some food at home?" Crista asked when they were passing around McDonald's.

"Yeah, why not?" Kenesta nodded; she wasn't in the mood to cook, and some fast food sounded good at this moment.

"Great," Crista said as she led the way to the door. They went to the self-kiosk to order. Kenesta chose a burger with chips and coke, and Crista took a wrap as well, with chips but with Sprite.

They waited for their food. Then, they continued home, where they ate it without much speaking. And as it was starting to be late, Kenesta went to prepare for bed. In the shower, she washed her hair, and her thoughts swam back to the image.

Her thoughts were with her family. During meditation, she decided to try to contact someone from her world. If she was successful, she would tell them about this world and about Crista. She didn't know if it would work, but it was her only option for contacting someone, and she needed it.

She got out of the shower and dried quickly. Then, she almost ran to the bedroom because she didn't want to wait. She didn't even notice that her hair dried instantly as she used her magic. She entered the room and immediately took a sitting position in the middle of the room and started.

It didn't take her long to get to her space, and then she thought about her friend. She imagined the faces of all of her friends and wished to speak with them the same way they used with Crista. It didn't appear to be working for a few moments. But then she felt pulled at her core. She could see a rope attached to it. She didn't know where the rope was coming from, but it should be a good sign.

She went near the rope and tried to send a message, "Is someone there?"

For a moment, it looked like nothing happened. She wanted to give up. But then she heard a small voice coming from the rope.

"Ken, is that you?" Kenesta wasn't sure who the voice was, but it was one of her friends for sure.

"Yes, that's me," she said excitedly.

The voice said, "Ken, where are you? Everyone is looking for you."

"I'm not entirely certain. It is a new world, but don't worry, I am fine. How are you?"

"How did you get there?"

"I don't know. I remember being with my family, and then I woke up in the hospital in this world."

"Okay, we'll find a way to get you back here. Don't worry." At this point, Kenesta recognised the voice as her vampire friend Clotie.

"No, don't worry about me. I am fine. I found a good friend here, and she is teaching me about this world. I am even learning their language. It is not disrespectful here. And they have music that they play in these small boxes. It's amazing here; I wish you could be here with me to see it," Kenesta said, hoping her friend would understand.

"Sounds nice, but you need to come back; we miss you. Your family is worried that something has happened to you. You have to find your soulmate; you can't stay there," Clotie stated emphatically. But Kenesta didn't want to leave Crista in this world alone. And she was sure that she and Crista were soulmates. It was the feeling.

But she was at a loss for words. She wanted to argue and fight but didn't know how.

"No buts, we will find a way, don't worry," was the last thing the voice said as the rope broke in the middle.

Kenesta stood there for a few more minutes. She was afraid to leave this space and discover that she had appeared in her world. But then she heard Crista calling her, and she decided to wake up to see what she needed.

Kenesta opened her eyes and saw Crista standing in front of her. Crista looked worried. Not like in the restaurant, but she is still concerned about what happened to her.

"Is everything alright, Kenesta?" Crista asked.

Kenesta lied. "Yeah, I was meditating," she said. She didn't want to tell her about her talk with Clotie.

"Are you sure? I thought I heard your voice and someone else," Crista said unimpressed. "They were speaking about going back to your world."

Kenesta was shocked that Crista was able to hear the conversation. She had no idea how it was possible. "I don't want to talk about it now. Can we leave it for another time?"

"Yeah, of course, just remember, I'm here for you," Crista said, kissing her on the forehead before she left the room. Kenesta didn't know how to react. All this dating stuff was new for her. She liked Crista, but she didn't know anything about dating.

Chapter 7

Kenesta woke up the next day earlier than usual. She felt more tired than when she went to sleep. It was because of dreams about her family and friends. The air was thick with hushed whispers. They filled her ears. Each was a testament to the worry that hung in the air. She found herself at a loss, uncertain of her next course of action. She is at a crossroads. She is torn between returning to her old realm or staying with Crista.

She lay in bed and stared at the ceiling. Her thoughts scattered like leaves in the wind. They drifted aimlessly through her vast mind. Deliberating upon the merits and demerits of both realms. She contemplated the future. It includes the tangible realm we inhabit and the ethereal world beyond. Uncertain of Crista's desires regarding motherhood, she harboured no such inclination. Motherhood did not come naturally to her. The responsibility of tending to young ones was an intimidating endeavour. Another individual would soon find themselves relying on her. The object of her disdain was not to her liking.

In her world, having kids was a must. Displeasure coursed through her veins. She found herself with her family. They never stopped asking about her search for her soulmate and having kids. In this place, the anticipation of her actions was non-existent. In this new environment, she experienced a profound sense of liberation. However, a conflicting sentiment tugged at her heartstrings. The pangs of longing for her beloved family and cherished friends grew stronger. They cast a shadow over her firm spirit. The idea that they might worry for her well-being gnawed at her conscience. It left an indelible mark of unease.

She lay there for another minute. Then, she decided to prepare breakfast for her and Crista. Crista was supposed to go to work around midday. She didn't like to be left alone with her thoughts. But today Pav had lectures at the university, so they would meet tomorrow. Maybe she could go to the library alone and borrow some fantasy books. It would be nice to know a different view on magic than the one she knows.

In the kitchen, she grabbed some slices of bread and put them in the toaster to toast them on both sides. Then she grabbed some fresh avocados, cream cheese, and lemon. She mixed it together in a small bowl and started preparing fried eggs. This was Crista's favourite breakfast, and she wanted it to be perfect.

When the toast was ready, she put the avocados on top and then the eggs. Meanwhile, Crista woke up and came to the kitchen. She was observing Kenesta as she was preparing breakfast.

"It's looking good," she said as she walked slowly toward her.

Kenesta smiled and turned to Crista. She gave her one of the plates, and together they sat by the table. They ate quietly, as both of them were lost in their thoughts.

Kenesta's mind was still consumed by thoughts of her beloved family. Their faces were vividly etched in her memory. She couldn't help but dwell on the moments they had shared. The laughter and tears had woven the tapestry of their lives. The warmth of their presence lingered in her heart, even as she found herself in the midst of a new day. Meanwhile, Crista's mind was preoccupied with the delicate art of conversation. She pondered the events of yesterday. She searched for the perfect words to bridge the gap between then and now. How could she gently bring it up? She wanted to weave a smooth thread that would connect their shared experiences. Her thoughts were heavy. They urged her to find the right balance. She needed to balance curiosity and sensitivity. She was reluctant to force Kenesta into any situation that might cause her unease. But she still yearned to help her.

"What are your plans for today?" Crista asked when she finished her breakfast.

Kenesta didn't expect it, and she jumped on the voice in her head. She looked at Crista and just shrugged her shoulders, continuing with her breakfast. She didn't feel like saying anything to her, and she didn't have any plans yet.

"Is everything alright, Kenesta?" Crista was worried. Kenesta was usually happy, but she hadn't smiled today. "You know, you can tell me everything."

"Yeah, everything is fine," Kenesta said quietly. She knew she could trust Crista, but she didn't want to be a burden especially not after yesterday.

"I don't believe you," Crista said, and she sat closer. "Something is bothering you, and I want to help you. Please allow me to help you."

"Nothing's happening," Kenesta said, standing up from the table. She blocked their connection and left the room without another word.

Crista looked after Kenesta until she closed the door and put her head in her hands. She didn't know what to do. Something was bothering Kenesta, but she didn't want to share it with her and didn't know how to help her.

Maybe she could ask one of her co-workers who had more experience with dating. Maybe they would know what to do and would tell her how to approach the situation. As she decided, she checked the clock and saw that she still had two hours before she would need to go to work.

She went to the living room and turned on the television to see what was happening in the world. She was checking her social media on the phone. She wanted to post pictures of her and Kenesta. But she didn't have any. Kenesta didn't like posing for photos, and Crista understood as it was uncommon in her world.

Crista was listening to television and browsing social media. Kenesta was in her room reading one of the books Crista bought her to improve her English. This was yet another benefit for the world. She could learn as many languages as she wanted here, and it wasn't as offensive as it was in her home country. Learning about cultures, cuisine, and many more things was different. In her world, varied species hid their cultures and didn't allow anyone to learn about them.

After a moment, she decided to go to the library. She would find some fantasy books. She would spend time there alone, free from her intrusive family's thoughts. She changed into a dress and went out. She could hear the television from the living room, but she didn't react to it and just quietly left the flat.

She was hurrying to arrive before it got too crowded. She was worried she wouldn't find an armchair. When she arrived at the library, she went to the fiction section. She looked for books with fantasy themes. A couple sounded interesting, but she wanted the one with magic and they should be like her situation.

She found books by an author named Rick Riordan, who wrote something like this, but it was in this modern world. She decided to give it a shot; if she didn't like it, she'd look for another one later. She took the book, which appeared to be the first in the series, and sat down. In a couple of moments, she was lost in the story and didn't pay attention to her surroundings.

Crista was watching television until she had to leave for work. She changed her clothes into her uniform. Then, she decided to look at Kenesta. But when she opened her doors, the room was empty. Crista was surprised, as she didn't hear her leave, but she put herself behind her and left the flat. She would contact Kenesta later if she didn't show up.

Crista came to work exactly on time. The restaurant wasn't busy at all. There was only one table of customers who were currently eating their lunch. Crista went behind the bar, where she left her stuff. She said hi to her colleague. She would be working with him today.

"Who is the chef today?"

"David," her colleague said lazily.

"Good, I'll say hello to him," Crista said as she walked into the kitchen. She liked it when David was working. He was leaving lots of food for the staff. And when someone asked for something specific, he had no problem making it. And he was also the best listener and adviser. So, Crista wanted to speak with him about her problem with Kenesta.

"Hi!" Crista yelled when she came into the kitchen. She wanted to be heard by everyone in the kitchen.

"Hi, Crista, how is my favourite waitress?" Behind the hot plate, the chef smiled.

"All right, what are you making today?" She asked, smiling.

"Would you like some bacon and leek pies and lasagne for a break?"

"Sure thing."

"Perfect. Now tell me about your new object. I heard from others that you started dating someone. I want to know all the details." David loved gossip; sometimes he was worse than any woman, but Crista liked him for it.

"Oh, you know, it's pretty new," she smiled.

"How did you meet? Did you kiss already? Did you mention sex?"

Crista had to laugh; he was like the high school girl who lived only for dramas.

"You know my opinion about sex, Dave."

"I do, but you never know." He winked at her, and Crista had to laugh more.

"I'll tell you all the details after work. We can get some drinks and talk about her. What do you think?"

"Sure thing, I want to know everything, dear Crista."

"Great, see you later. I have to go back to work." Crista left the kitchen and went back behind the bar. The restaurant stayed quiet.

Crista was cleaning the restaurant. It was one of those calm days. The patrons seemed to have chosen to arrive later. This left the establishment in a state of serene stillness. So far, only five tables had been arranged for the day. A sixth table would be set for the evening. The anticipation of a rush lingered in the air. It was as if the restaurant craved the lively energy about to come. Yet, if the evening failed to bring many customers, the calm of the day would continue. It would be unbroken and undisturbed.

At six, Crista took her break. Dave prepared one of the pies with potato mash, carrots, beets, Brussels sprouts, and lots of gravy. Crista liked gravy so much that she was putting it on everything.

When Crista went on her break, Dave delegated his job to the sous chef and told him to call him if things got too busy. Dave could then join Crista on her break. They could freely talk about her new relationship.

They sat by one of the outside tables, and meanwhile, Crista was eating. She was telling David all about her new relationship. She told him about the fear she had before and about the last night. Dave was listening to her and waiting until she finished to ask questions. He was curious about Kenesta and asked what she liked and where she was from. Crista tried to answer as best she could, as she didn't want to reveal anything true about her world.

"To me," Dave started, "it seems that she is lost in her feelings. She is likely unsure what she wants. When she gets the call from her country, her feelings surface. Now, she doesn't know if she wants to stay or go home. She just needs time to sort through her emotions and set her priorities. As you said, it's her first relationship."

"Yeah, she hasn't been dating before," Crista confirmed.

"Well, that also means she doesn't know what it is. I would recommend starting slowly. When you get home, make her dinner, or I can cook something for you, and then you can watch some movies or play games. Simply show her that you take her seriously. The moving-in together was too quick, I would say, but it was before you started dating, so this doesn't matter. Just try to give her some space to express herself, and it should be fine. And I want to see updates," Dave said. He stood up and left Crista with her thoughts.

In a moment of clarity, she saw the importance of giving Kenesta the freedom to explore her desires. She also saw the importance of her finding her voice. Yet, she couldn't stop her desire to help her. She wanted to help her navigate her thoughts. Thus, she remained seated, patiently awaiting the end of her shift. As the minutes ticked by, she tried to occupy herself with tasks. But sadly, the restaurant and bar stayed calm all day.

Dave was still there and offered to give Crista a lift home, as he was going the same way and was concerned about her. She agreed, and together they went to Dave's car. They usually went home together. Some waitstaff thought she and Dave were dating. But, neither of them said anything about it. They let the rumour spread and then just laughed about the stupidity.

Dave was married and had two kids, and Crista was an ace and a lesbian. They were always together. They laughed at the remaining staff and talked about the thoughts and theories of the poor. Today was the same.

"What do you think she thought when we left?" Dave started.

"Maybe where are we going to fuck today? If it's your place or mine," Crista smirked.

"It should be, or if we have a threesome with your new girlfriend," Dave said with a smile.

"That's for sure," she said, smiling at the thought.

Dave dropped Crista off at her flat, but it looked like no one was home. The flat was dark and cold. Crista went to Kenesta's room to see if she was sleeping but she wasn't there. Crista was having bad feelings; Kenesta should have been home by now, as it was almost nine o'clock.

Kenesta spent her whole day in the library reading books from Rick. His talent for creating complex worlds and weaving engaging stories was unmatched. It left her completely enthralled. One of his ideas resonated deeply with her. It was the idea of adding more deities. Though her realm had many goddesses but this parallel struck a chord within her. Moreover, in her own cherished realm, a young boy embarked on an extraordinary odyssey. He was blissfully unaware of an alternate reality. He ultimately discovered his divine lineage. But this truth would forever remain just a figment of imagination.

As the clock neared nine, a librarian approached her. She gave a gentle reminder that the library would soon close. She urged her to say goodbye to the books and go home. Kenesta was grateful for the librarian's thoughtfulness. She expressed her thanks before gently closing the book she had been reading. She returned it to the shelves and decided to go home. Crista probably finished her shift and would be home soon.

After reading a captivating novel, she resolved to confide in her friend. She wanted to share about the heavy burdens on her mind. Like the protagonist in the book, she found solace in the unwavering support of loyal friends. She also trusted Crista's ability to listen with empathy. Her trust was unwavering. Sharing one's worries with trusted friends was meaningful. It fostered a bond built on vulnerability and mutual understanding.

The way home was quiet. She liked the evening walks through the city. Unless it was Wednesday and university students were out, there weren't many people. But today, there were only a couple of people, and Kenesta loved it. Because of that, the trip home took her almost forty minutes.

When she was near the house, she could see lights in the flat, which meant that Crista was already home from work. Kenesta didn't know how she got there so quickly, but she knew that she was probably worrying about her.

She started walking faster to be home quickly. She ran through the stars and opened the door. Crista was behind them, putting her jacket back on, and when she heard the door open, she turned. Kenesta could see the relief on her face at finally seeing her.

"Where were you?" Crista asked. She asked right away when Kenesta opened the telepathic connection between them.

"In the library, I found a really good book and forgot about time."

Crista simply nodded and removed her jacket, saying, "Ok, but please let me know next time; I was worried about you."

"Yes, of course." Kenesta smiled at her. She knew that next time she would let her know.

"Come, you have to be starving. Dave gave me some leftovers," Crista said. She led them to the kitchen. There were two bags full of food.

"That sounds good," Kenesta said, smiling, and sitting down by the table.

Crista prepared two plates. She took out one of the containers. Inside were roasted vegetables: carrots, parsley, Brussels sprouts, and potatoes. She put some of each on the plates and took out another container with cauliflower cheese. She put a generous portion on each plate.

"Do you want beef or pork?" Crista asked when she would open the third container.

"Beef, please," Kenesta said, and Crista put sliced roasted beef on one plate and pork on another. Then she took out the container with gravy and spilt it over the food. Lastly, she took out Yorkshire puddings and put them on the plates. When she was done, she put the plates on the table. Meanwhile, Kenesta summoned cutlery.

They ate in silence, both lost in their thoughts. Kenesta was thinking about ways to tell Crista about her worries. She was also thinking about how to apologise to her. Crista was thinking about what Dave told her and how to approach Kenesta about it.

Kenesta took the plates and put them in the sink when they finished. When she waved her hand, the plates were clean again.

"You can do magic again." Crista smiled at the way Kenesta was practising magic with ease.

"Yeah, it feels so good to be able to do it again. I felt worthless without it," Kenesta smiled. She cleaned the whole kitchen in a different way.

"That's good."

"Also, I want to apologise for yesterday," Kenesta started, "because I was scared as I didn't know what I really wanted."

"And now do you know it?"

"No, but I don't want to make the decision alone," Kenesta said, shaking her head.

"And you will not. I am here for you."

"Thank you." Crista hugged Kenesta. They stood there for a few moments, thinking about the future and what might happen there.

"Can you tell me what exactly happened yesterday?" Crista asked. Kenesta nodded. She told her about her talk with her friend and their disagreement.

"That will be alright. We are in it together," Crista told her without breaking the hug.

"Thanks, I appreciate it."

"Of course," Crista kissed Kenesta's forehead. "Do you want to watch TV, or do you want to go to sleep?"

"Can we watch some fantasy movies, please?" Kenesta asked with puppy eyes.

"Of course, what about Harry Potter?" Crista asked. She was thinking about all the magic in the movies.

"All right," Kenesta said, despite the fact that she had never seen the film. Crista smiled. Together they went to the living room. There, Crista found the DVD of Harry Potter and the Philosopher's Stone. She put it in her laptop so they could be close together and have the laptop on their laps.

Kenesta sat captivated. Her eyes fixed on the opening scenes of the movie. She found herself grappling with the unfathomable reality of the wizarding world. It was as if a veil had been lifted. It revealed a realm of enchantment and wonder. She had never before dared to imagine it. She wondered could this mystical realm truly exist. Did the people in her world not know about it? The magic she saw on the screen resonated deeply within her. It struck a chord of familiarity she couldn't quite explain. Yet, unlike the wizards and witches portrayed in the film, Kenesta had never wielded a wand. Nowhere in the history of magic had she read of people with magical powers but no way to channel them through a wand. It was a perplexing conundrum. It left her pondering the details of this amazing universe.

Kenesta told Crista about her thoughts, but Crista just laughed.

"This is pure fiction; there is no magic in this world."

"If there is no magic, how am I doing magic? Or how we talk to each other; this is also magic. And in a world without magic, I would be unable to do it."

"Maybe there is some, but this is just a story."

It was the final word about the magic from Crista, but Kenesta didn't want to believe it. There must be a wizarding community. It was probably different from in this movie, but there had to be some.

For the rest of the film, Kenesta ignored the plot and focused on how to locate a wizard community in this world. Maybe this thing out there, or whatever it is, could help her. The library could have some useful books about it.

After the movie, Kenesta went into her bedroom and prepared to go to bed. She didn't meditate. She was scared. She feared she would talk to someone else. They would bother her when she returned to her world. But before she went to sleep, she took her phone and started searching.

She typed 'wizard community' into Google's search engine and hoped for the best. And it did. Mostly, they were historical accounts. They were tales of women accused of practising the dark arts. Yet, amidst these sombre narratives, a flicker of promise emerged. Like a beacon in the night, she stumbled upon websites that spoke of natural and elemental magic. The portals were digital. They held the potential to unlock the secrets she sought so desperately. At that moment, she realised that some fervently believed in magic. They had the knowledge and power to aid her in her quest.

She didn't meditate. When she fell asleep, her mind moved to her magic core and connected with someone. Kenesta thought she would never speak at all. It was the first time she dreamed about their goddess and the first time she was able to speak with her.

"My dear Kenesta, I am so happy to see you." A lady in her mid-thirties stood in front of Kenesta. She wore simple white robes and a diadem in her hair. She didn't have any shoes. Her long, dark hair was in a braid.

"Your Majesty," Kenesta said, bowing. She didn't know how to react.

"My child, you don't need to be formal; I am here to see how you are. When you disappeared, everyone thought it was scary and prayed for your return. But I couldn't help because, as you know, you're needed here," the goddess explained.

"What do you mean?" Kenesta was confused.

"You are needed here, as your soulmate is in this world."

"So is Crista my soulmate?" Kenesta wanted to know. She liked the girl and wanted to be happy with her.

The goddess just smiled and nodded. Kenesta felt the joy of the confirmation. She was happy she found her, and she probably wouldn't need to leave her now.

"So does that mean I can stay here with her?"

"Well, that's a bit of a problem. You don't belong to this world," the goddess started. "Crista cannot go with you, as she doesn't belong there." Then, all the joy left. "But there is a solution to this problem, but I can't tell you more; you will have to figure it out yourself."

It was her final words before she vanished, leaving Kenesta alone.

Over the next few days, Kenesta immersed herself in the captivating pursuit. She sought to unravel the secrets of the wizarding community. She did this within this enchanting world. Each day, she went on a pilgrimage to the hallowed halls of the library. There, she delved deep into its vast knowledge reservoir. She searched its resources. She did so in her quest to understand the mystical realm of wizards and witches. At times, she was with her new friend, Pavlina. Pavlina helped her learn about magic and improve her English.

One day, she decided to ask her about her country, maybe they had a different view than Britain. Pavlina was initially a bit sceptical. She pondered the reason for Kenesta's curiosity. However, she eventually succumbed to the allure of sharing. She then divulged details about her beloved Czechia. She explained its captivating natural wonders and rich cultural tapestry.

To Kenesta, this country sounded amazing. From her talking, she could feel that there had to be a wizarding community. Because of the nature, the culture was also similar to one clan in her world. There was a huge possibility she found someone who would be able to help her.

The days were passing quickly. Kenesta forgot her talk with her friend and started to meditate again. Each day, her magic grew stronger. She dedicated herself to honing her skills during the day. It was during one such moment that she found her new ability. She could transfigure her bed into a small, loyal dog. It provided her with much-needed company.

Crista saw the change and she was happy for her. She knew how Kenesta missed her magic and watching her practise was exciting. But she wasn't used to it when something changed in the flat or when music played from nowhere. But she didn't mind.

Kenesta kept searching for the communities in the middle of Europe. She found many myths and tales. Her curiosity grew more every time she found new information. After two weeks of research, she spoke with Crista about an idea she had for a while.

"Crista, can we speak about something?" Kenesta started.

"Sure, what do you want to speak about?" Crista looked at her.

"I was thinking if we could go to visit Czechia. The country sounds amazing, and I would like to see more from this world when I am here."

Her request startled Crista. She hadn't thought of going on holiday for a long time and Kenesta already thinking about leaving her. The question sounded like she knew, she would have to go back to her world.

"I guess we can go, but I don't know when I'll get annual leave as the work is busy right now."

"That's fine. We can go for just two days. It doesn't have to be a long visit. I just want to see the country and visit some city there."

"Okay, that could be alright then. I'll speak with my boss. Then we can plan something," Crista said. She was already thinking about how to ask her boss and where to book a flight. Maybe they could use some of the low-cost airlines to save some money.

"That's great, thanks," Kenesta smiled and hugged Crista. Kenesta was already planning what she wanted to visit. She had found some magical parts in the country, and she needed to check them. She hoped she was in the right way to find out how she could stay here. Especially when the goddess didn't specify anything for her.

The next day, Crista went to work and Kenesta stood in the apartment alone. She turned her bed into a small dog and went into the living room to watch something on the TV. However, she spent most of the time on the phone looking for new places to visit, if Czechia wouldn't work.

She found a mention of Native Americans. They still believed in the gods. Maybe it would be useful to visit and ask about her situation. But it would take hours on the plane to get to America. They would also need more than two days to find some of these people.

Kenesta started to write a list of places she thought would be good to visit. They were the most mythical places in the Czech Republic. However, what she truly sought were not just physical destinations. She wanted vibrant communities full of life. Still, she couldn't help, but ponder the intriguing scenarios. They might unfold once she and her friends set foot in these mystical realms.

Crista came from work early today and she was smiling.

"Kenesta, we can go next week. I got three days off in a row. Let's go book tickets," Crista said outside the flat by telepathy.

"Great," Kenesta jumped happily in her seat and scared the dog who was lying in her lap. Before Crista entered the flat, she was already searching for plane tickets and hotels. She did this even though she didn't know which day Crista got off.

Crista went inside. She could see Kenesta focused on searching flights and other stuff on her phone.

"I was thinking of taking Lynx Airline. It's cheap and we could catch them from Birmingham Airport." Crista looked at Kenesta and she nodded. It sounded good. If they save money on the plane, they can have more experience in the place.

"Okay, but I think there will be one problem. I don't have identification documents," Kenesta started. But before she could finish her thoughts, on the table there appeared a British passport.

Crista and Kenesta exchanged looks. Crista grabbed the passport from the table to see who it belonged to and she couldn't believe her eyes. The passport was for Kenesta, and the last name was Klistia.

"Is your last name Klistia?" Crista asked her.

"What's last name?" Kenesta asked confused.

"Your family name," Crista explained.

"I don't have any of these. But Klistia means female leader in my language, and it is the name of our Goddess."

"Strange. But at least the problem with documents is solved."

Kenesta's face lit up with a radiant smile; her heart brimming with gratitude. It was a relief to have found someone willing to help. They were spared the hard task of devising an escape plan to return her safely to the United Kingdom. With new hope, the girls spent the rest of the evening focused on getting tickets. They also arranged a place to stay for their long-awaited weekend trip.

They booked a flight from Birmingham Airport early in the morning. They did this to get there with plenty of time. For the same reason, they booked their return flight for late in the evening. Kenesta liked this idea. They booked two hotels, to see as much as possible. One was in the capital city. The second was in another city in the south. Kenesta read that there was a possibility to find a secret community.

Chapter 8

The days before the flight seemed to fly by. Kenesta's excitement for the trip grew and she couldn't contain it. The day before, she excitedly discussed her plans. She talked about the many places she hoped to explore.

Her excitement was palpable. She tossed and turned the night before the flight, unable to sleep. Finally, at three in the morning, she gave up. She went to the kitchen to brew coffee for herself and Crista. They had to leave before four to ensure they arrived at the airport by six. They completed the check-in the day before. They took extra care to ensure they had the tickets.

Crista shared all the details about flying. She also covered the needed preparations. They would need to go through security and passport control. Then, they would board their flight to the continent. Kenesta embraced each step with joy. She was eager to start a new endeavour. In her world, there are no planes and people could not fly without wings or the ability to fly. The experience was unlike any other. She longed to see the planet from space. They made sure to reserve two seats together, with one of them being a window seat for Kenesta.

When Crista woke up, she looked like she had just left a restless sleep. Dark circles adorned the area under her eyes. As she made her way to the kitchen, a cup of coffee materialised before her, courtesy of Kenesta. She gave a gracious nod to show appreciation. Then, she began to savour the warm drink, taking her time with each sip. She wasn't a morning person, and this was too early for her, but she was willing to make sacrifices for Kenesta.

As she savoured her coffee, a wave of rejuvenation washed over her. She glanced at Kenesta, who sat across from her, wearing a wide grin.

"Have you managed to get any sleep?" Crista asked. But Kenesta shook her head in response, keeping her cheerful expression.

Crista remarked that it would be a long day for Kenesta. Kenesta simply nodded in agreement. "Well, it seems that one of us is content in the early hours of the day."

"Don't be so grumpy, you're going to love it," Kenesta said with great enthusiasm.

"Well, waking up at this hour should definitely be against the law."

"Oh, come on," Kenesta chuckled. She found it amusing when Crista complained about mornings.

Once they finished their coffees, they gathered their things. Then they made their way to the vehicle. Crista would drive the whole journey. They planned to park the car at the airport. It would be waiting there for them when they returned.

The car journey was fortunately short, with minimal traffic along the way. The entire journey lasted approximately one hour, so they arrived at the parking lot at 5 a.m. They had ample time to catch the fly since it departed at 8:25 a.m. Crista was hoping to leave earlier. She was worried about traffic or any unexpected events during the journey to the airport.

Crista retrieved her backpack from the car. She confidently stated, "Alright, our next task is to get past security. Then, we can have a tasty breakfast before our flight." Kenesta nodded and eagerly grabbed her bag. She gazed upon the magnificent structure of the airport.

The structure in front of her was a masterpiece of new architecture. Its magnificence was unaffected by the dim lighting. Her heart raced with excitement as she gazed upon an aeroplane for the very first time. Crista made a promise to show her take-offs and landings. She would do so before the actual flight.

As they entered, a vibrant and lively scene came into view. The air crackled with an electric buzz. A diverse crowd formed orderly lines. They were barely able to contain their excitement. They were all waiting to check in. The room buzzed with people, each one seated and seemingly lost in their own thoughts. They exuded a sense of quiet anticipation. It was their turn to pass through security or to reunite with loved ones. Kenesta was uncertain. She had never seen the hustle and bustle of an airport. They ascended the grand staircase with purpose. She and Crista made their way to the second floor. They had a firm destination in mind. Amidst the hallowed halls, security personnel stood guard, diligently protecting the premises.

Upstairs, a massive queue of people stretched out before them. A group of individuals stood at the forefront. They wore immaculate uniforms and exuded an undeniable aura of authority. The travellers were in a line. They were met by a big group of metal structures. Kenesta and Crista entered the queue. Their spot was secured among the busy crowd. Crista calmly told Kenesta to get the liquids. They were in her reliable rucksack. Kenesta listened intently, her eyes brimming with curiosity. She skilfully reached for the plastic bag. It held a collection of creams and serums. Kenesta added these potions to her daily skincare routine with religious devotion. She followed this sacred practice with care at home. She carefully arranged the elements: the bag, the jacket, and the other items. She put them on a plain plastic tray.

They carefully carried the tray with them as they gracefully moved in front of the queue. Kenesta was uncertain about what to expect when they found themselves in the front. She observed a group of people. The metallic figures made strange noises. The uniformed people promptly escorted the group away. She was filled with fear, uncertain of how she would respond if that situation were to occur. Perhaps they would deny her the chance to journey. They might find that she did not truly fit in this realm.

As they approached the conveyor belt, a figure in a crisp uniform awaited their tray. The individual politely asked if they had any electronic devices in their possession. Crista declined the offer politely and gracefully. Undeterred, the person continued to place their belongings into yet another metallic contraption. Kenesta stood frozen, her gaze locked onto her bag as it slowly disappeared into the distance. She was engulfed by a wave of uncertainty, leaving her at a loss for what to do next. She followed Crista with a sense of admiration; her gaze captivated by her every action. Crista exuded self-assurance. She guided the group to the mysterious metal structure that loomed ahead. A mysterious figure hid in the shadows. They extended their hand gracefully, inviting

Crista to come closer. Their eyes connected. A small smile danced on her lips. She glided past Kenesta with effortless grace.

Crista was in a state of anticipation. She patiently waited for something to occur. The person waved at Kenesta, causing her to feel a surge of nervousness as she walked through. She anticipated the noise and glided past it. But it remained silent. This granted her the freedom to continue.

"Well, it wasn't as bad as expected," Crista said to herself. Kenesta approached her.

"Yeah, I thought, they arrested me," Kenesta nodded.

"They wouldn't, don't worry. Now, let's grab our things and go get some breakfast," Crista said with a smile. Kenesta nodded in agreement. The two of them gracefully retrieved their backpacks from the strange metal device. With a sense of purpose, they set off on a quest. They aimed to find a quaint coffee shop or a charming restaurant where they could eat.

They made their way through the duty-free shop. Many enticing products awaited them. Perfumes, alcohol, and a myriad of other items were on display, beckoning to be explored. Kenesta decided to take a moment to explore her surroundings. However, upon seeing Crista was tired, she decided to go with her to a busy area. It was filled with shops and cosy coffee places. Everywhere, television screens displayed the departure flights. Kenesta was filled with awe. She saw the sheer number of flights departing from the airport and the bustling crowd of people.

"What is the maximum capacity of a plane in terms of passenger count?" She asked Crista.

"Well, the size of the plane is a determining factor. There are smaller options for less than a hundred people. And medium-sized ones for around two hundred people. Then, there's the larger one for up to six hundred," Crista explained as she scanned the area for a place to eat.

After a few minutes, Crista suggested going to Costa. She confidently led them to the Costa coffee shop at the far end of the hall.

Kenesta nodded. She obediently trailed behind Crista. They were heading to a cluster of small stands in the busy marketplace. There was already a queue of people patiently waiting for their coffee. Crista joined the queue and instructed Kenesta to locate a table for the two of them. Kenesta surveyed her surroundings. Her eyes landed on a secluded corner of the 'garden' for Costa customers. She ventured there without a second thought.

"Would you like something to drink as well?" Crista asked, using telepathy.

"Sure, I'll have a caramel latte please," Kenesta replied taking a seat at the table she had selected.

Fifteen minutes later, Crista arrived at the table. She carried two cups of coffee and two freshly toasted Paninis. Kenesta expressed her thanks. Then, she savoured one of the Paninis, delighting in each bite.

Crista suggested that, after we're done, we could go to the duty-free shop. We have plenty of time before our flight.

"Hmm," Kenesta nodded with her mouth full of food. She was already enamoured with this journey.

"Have you ever wondered if we see an aeroplane before it soars?" Kenesta asked as she swallowed.

"Certainly, I did promise to show you some take-offs and landings before we depart, didn't I?" Crista agreed.

Kenesta smiled, expressing her approval.

They savoured their breakfast, basking in the moment for about twenty minutes. Kenesta was keenly observing the individuals in their vicinity. Observing people's behaviour, shopping habits, or simply eavesdropping on their conversations. She discovered details about their upcoming vacation. When they were done, Crista graciously collected their used cups. She carried them to the spot for dirty dishes.

"Alright, let's get going."

Kenesta trailed behind her as they made their way back to the duty-free shop. She examined the cosmetics, intrigued by the ones she hadn't heard of before. Crista decided to try a few different perfumes. She kindly offered Kenesta the chance to experience them too.

"Are you planning on buying something?" Kenesta asked. She had carefully sampled many perfumes.

"Indeed, I need a new one for work. But I am unsure which one would be best," Crista acknowledged with a nod.

"I prefer the one in the black bottle with the circle in the middle."

"Yes, that scent is nice. But I was actually considering this one," Crista said as she reached for another bottle of perfume. The bottle had a striking resemblance to a robot donning a pair of stylish sunglasses. She sprayed a small amount onto a piece of paper, giving it a quick shake before handing it to Kenesta to take a whiff.

She nodded in approval, acknowledging the pleasant aroma. Crista offered a warm smile. She graciously accepted the sealed box of perfume.

"Would you like something?" Crista asked about Kenesta's interest in a skincare product.

Kenesta expressed her interest in trying the cream with a hint of shyness.

"Not at all," Crista smiled, enjoying the opportunity to pamper Kenesta.

"I appreciate it. However, it is quite costly, and you are already covering all expenses."

"I've already mentioned that money isn't a problem," Crista said casually. She said she had enough money to lead a comfortable life for the next five decades.

Kenesta nodded and eagerly picked up the cream she had been longing to try.

"Once we return, I'll also begin my job search. It could help my English," Kenesta said. They strolled towards the cashier to pay.

"If you want to, but remember, it's not necessary."

"Yes, I understand, but I have a strong desire to do so."

Crista simply nodded and offered a warm smile to Kenesta. She understood the root of her desire to work. But it wasn't mainly for her own benefit. Perhaps they could assist her in securing a position at a quaint coffee shop or a charming bookstore. She desires a place where she can be surrounded by others yet find it engaging and effortless.

They paid for their stuff and took a leisurely stroll around the terminal. Kenesta was eager to catch a glimpse of the planes before the boarding process began. With at least an hour to spare, they had plenty of time to satisfy their curiosity. During the stroll, Crista got a notification about their gate. She quickly checked the designated location. They decided to head in that direction, not too far from where they were. As they made their way, they couldn't help but pause by a window. From there, they caught a glimpse of a plane gracefully taking off into the sky.

Kenesta was captivated by the scene unfolding before her. She pressed her face to the glass with childlike wonder. She eagerly watched the huge machine glide along the ramp. And then, in a breathtaking moment, it ascended into the vast expanse of the sky. She was captivated by the breathtaking view. She longed to be aboard the plane, craving a firsthand encounter. Kenesta gazed at the plane, captivated by its presence. Meanwhile, Crista discreetly moved a few steps away. She skilfully took a candid snapshot of Kenesta. She adored capturing moments of Kenesta's excitement. She also loved it when Kenesta was fully engrossed in something new.

They stayed in that spot for a few minutes. Then, they went to their gate. They patiently occupied their seats, eagerly anticipating the commencement of the boarding process. Crista used Flight Radar to check the flight details. She was able to view info about the aircraft. She noticed the plane arriving from Prague and preparing for its return journey. And she noticed that they would arrive at least twenty minutes early.

Crista glanced at Kenesta. Kenesta was engrossed in her phone, searching for information on aeroplanes. Crista knew they would fly on a Boeing 737. It was the only aircraft used by the airline.

"Flight ST2014 to Prague is ready for priority boarding at gate 25. Please prepare your boarding pass and travel documents in picture size for check. We would like to remind you that priority passengers can take one big bag, one small and one bag of duty-free. Other passengers are allowed only one small bag and one bag of duty-free. Additional or bigger luggage will be checked in and brought to cargo." The announcement echoed through the gate. Passengers began to form two lines. They were preparing to check in bigger or extra bags for the cargo hold. Kenesta quickly stood up and asserted her importance. She turned to Crista, who just chuckled and rose from her seat.

Crista handed over her phone. It held both boarding passes and their passports. She did this when it was their turn. The woman graciously accepted them, her face lighting up with a warm smile. She carefully examined the boarding passes. She compared the names on the passports to ensure they matched perfectly. She handed them back to Crista, wishing them a safe journey.

The passengers had to get off the aircraft. They had to walk down the stairs to exit. The airline had opted to use their own stairs for boarding. They utilised both doors to expedite their movements. Before stepping outside, they found themselves in a brief interlude. They were waiting patiently. They waited for the last flight's passengers to leave and for the plane to be cleaned. Only then could they embark on their own journey.

Crista made sure to inspect their seats before they left. She figured out which door would be best to use. They were seated in row 2EF. The front door was absolutely magnificent. As they stepped outside, Crista gently grasped Kenesta's hand. She held it tightly as they made their way towards the aeroplane. Kenesta was innocent, like a young child. Her eyes were filled with curiosity as she observed her surroundings.

They ascended the staircase. As they stepped inside, they were greeted by two cabin crew members—one male and one female. The female crew member had a warm smile on her face, making them feel welcome. Crista glanced upwards and noticed the row numbers. Number two was just beyond a partition. Crista graciously guided Kenesta to her seat, ensuring her comfort without hesitation. Kenesta settled into the window seat, her gaze drawn to the world beyond the glass. Crista deftly got their backpacks and put them in the overhead compartment. There was no space nearby.

"Wow!" Kenesta exclaimed with a beaming smile. She turned to Crista, full of excitement.

She chuckled softly and planted a gentle kiss on Kenesta's forehead. Crista turned towards the guy behind them who had made a disgusted sound.

"Do you have any problem?"

"It is concerning how individuals such as yourself can roam freely. Perhaps it would be more appropriate for you to be confined, as your behaviour is far from ordinary."

"Pardon me!" Crista rose from her seat, compelled to share something with him. But a vigilant cabin crew member intercepted her intentions. They promptly approached to investigate.

"Is everything alright here?" The female cabin crew inquired.

"No," the man behind them objected. "These two individuals shouldn't be soaring through the skies; they should be behind bars."

"Sir, this behaviour is not acceptable by this airline. If you want to fly with us, keep your thoughts to yourself or you will have to leave," the cabin crew said.

"I refuse to stay silent. Those two engage in public displays of affection," he exclaimed, seething with anger.

"Alright, sir, this is your final opportunity to board the flight today. If you don't take it, you'll have to remain here."

"I paid for the ticket, so it is unjust for you to remove me from the flight!" He said, filled with anger.

"So, if you wish to soar, kindly avoid using these derogatory words." The crew departed, yet she continued to gaze in their direction. The man fell silent, his eyes filled with a look of disdain as he observed them.

Nothing eventful occurred for the remainder of the boarding process. Once boarding was finished, a female cabin crew member took charge. She captured everyone's attention as she confidently shut the door at the front of the plane. The gesture held deep symbolism, signifying the shift from planning to execution. The engines came alive with a gentle hum, and the cabin crew began their safety demonstration. Kenesta watched the male cabin crew with great curiosity. He carefully showed the passengers the location of the emergency exits. He also showed them how to fasten their seatbelts. Then, he went through all the necessary safety procedures. She contemplated the reasons behind their actions. A cloak of mystery covered their intentions.

"Do you have any idea about the reason behind this?" Kenesta inquired of Crista.

"To ensure our safety and be prepared in case of any unforeseen events," she responded.

The male cabin crew approached them. They did so once the passengers had finished. The crew guided them to their life jackets and safety cards. A warm smile spread across his face as he observed that everything in their row was in order. As he prepared to depart, the female cabin crew approached them. With an empty seat beside them, she leaned down and spoke in a hushed tone:

"If anything happens or if he troubles you, just press the call bell. We will be there to help you. Okay?"

"Thank you," Crista said with a smile. The cabin crew reciprocated the smiles and proceeded to make an announcement. When another crew member returned, she carefully inspected the cabin before take-off.

Kenesta remarked that the woman seemed nice. Crista responded with a nod and a smile. They were already making their way through the airport, nearing the ramp way.

"Are you prepared?" Crista enquired when the crew settled into their seats in front of the first row.

Kenesta smiled and gently took Crista's hand. She was excited as she gazed at the sky. But a rude man there refused to improve the situation.

Kenesta looked up at the expansive sky, her eyes brimming with awe. The celestial realm was mesmerising. It enthralled her and gave her comfort. It was a refuge in its boundless expanse. Meanwhile, inside the aircraft, the cabin crew were dedicated. They moved with elegance throughout the cabin, carefully doing their jobs. They were getting ready for the upcoming in-flight service. Kenesta stared out the window. Her gaze didn't move as she observed the ever-shifting landscape below. Meanwhile, Crista graciously accepted a magazine. A male cabin crew member had given it to her. Her eyes danced across the assortment of items before landing on a bottle of prosecco.

"How about we toast to the beginning of this journey with a bottle of prosecco?" Crista asked Kenesta.

"Sure, how many would you like?"

"Two and perhaps a few olives," Crista pondered, "is there anything else you would fancy?"

"No," Kenesta shook her head.

Crista nodded in agreement and patiently waited for the crew to begin their bar service.

Crista gracefully requested two bottles of prosecco. She asked for two olives and two bottles of water, which she promptly paid for.

The woman attending to them greeted them with a smile and handed over their belongings. She also helped Crista unveil the table. It had been cleverly hidden in the armrest.

Crista thanked them for their help. Then, she opened a bottle of prosecco. Carefully, she poured the sparkling wine into the plastic cups.

"Cheers," Crista exclaimed as she handed the second cup to Kenesta.

Kenesta smiled at her and took a small sip from the cup.

The man emitted a sound of disgust. Crista, however, chose to disregard it. She was determined to avoid another argument with him. Instead, she reached for her phone. She captured Kenesta's essence in a series of photos. Her smile was warm and genuine as she looked at her. As she tried to photograph their togetherness, a new cabin crew emerged. They caught sight of the scene.

"Would you like me to capture the moment for you?" She offered.

"Sure, thanks," Crista said, handing her the phone and moving closer to Kenesta. Kenesta leaned in and gently pressed her lips against Crista's cheek. It was a tender gesture that showed her affection.

The flight attendant returned the phone to Crista with a smile, exuding an air of perfection. They make a lovely couple.

"Thank you," Kenesta said with a smile. The man, however, chose to mutter once more about oddities. The observant cabin crew caught wind of his comments and promptly asked him to stop. However, he stubbornly continued to argue with the crew member. He passionately stated that such incidents should not be allowed on the aeroplane.

At that moment, the first flight attendant approached him again. She warned him that if he didn't stop, they would involve the authorities. He would be removed from the aircraft. He told them to give it a name. He knew they wouldn't catch him, but rather Crista with Kenesta.

The first cabin crew member glanced at her colleague. She told her to quickly contact the captain about the situation. It became clear that swift action was needed. The only choice was to tell the captain about the situation. And suddenly, his eyes were drawn to the young woman.

"Would you mind accompanying me to the galley? I have a few questions I'd like to discuss."

Crista gave a small nod before rising to her feet. But Kenesta couldn't shake off the fear of being caught, just as the man had warned. Crista offered a reassuring smile. She extended her hand and said everything would be alright. They discreetly slipped behind the wall, taking advantage of the cabin crew's permission. The second individual grabbed the interphone and appeared to be contacting the captain.

"Is everything okay?" The cabin crew inquired as soon as they disappeared from view.

Crista casually remarked, "Oh, we've grown accustomed to these comments by now."

"I understand the situation. But we have a zero-tolerance policy. It covers abuse and discrimination on the board. Therefore, we will be contacting the police." The cabin crew kindly told them that they could go to the police. They could file a criminal report if they wanted.

Crista hesitated at first, unsure if it was really needed. However, when she caught sight of Kenesta, struggling to hold back her tears, she knew she had to take action. She wanted to ensure that Kenesta didn't feel down on herself.

"Great, we will require your information since we need to compile a report for this. Please present your boarding passes and passports." Crista nodded in agreement. She then quickly got their documents and handed them to the flight attendant. She swiftly captured images and requested their contact information. They could then make their way back to their seats.

The crew members tried to continue with their tasks. But one of them fixated on the man in the third row. Kenesta was overwhelmed by the situation and longed to escape. But she found herself trapped with no way out. To find peace, she chose to shift her focus to the vast sky. She tuned out the chaos inside the cabin. She could have noticed the man's discreet actions. He stood up and headed to the restroom. During his journey back, he boldly aimed a venomous outburst at her. Crista was always watchful. She quickly noticed this malicious act. She firmly decided to protect Kenesta from future discrimination.

"What do you think you're doing?"

He sneered at her. He even spat on her, showing his complete disregard for what they deserved.

A fellow passenger quickly called for help by pressing the call bell. This got the attention of one of the alert cabin crew members. The front crew arrived promptly. They showed urgency that matched their position. She observed Crista in a heated argument with the man. A feeling of urgency swept over her. Without hesitation, she quickly extended her hand and pressed the call bell. This caused its chime to ring throughout the cabin not once or twice, but three times. A crew member quickly responded to her distress signal. They came from the depths of the aircraft and sprinted towards the unfolding scene.

The male cabin crew escorted the man to the rear of the plane. Meanwhile, Crista and Kenesta did their best. They tried to remain untouched by the commotion around them. One of the women went to get napkins so they could both clean up. The third crew went to contact the captain, presumably.

"Is everything okay?" The main cabin crew inquired of them.

Crista silently acknowledged the situation. She reached for the napkin to gently wipe away the saliva from Kenesta's face. She gazed out the window. She avoided eye contact with the person beside her.

She told them the man would stay in the back for the flight. Upon arrival, the police would escort him. Crista nodded, comprehending the situation. Another passenger spoke up. He told the cabin crew he wanted to act as a witness. He stressed the importance of such a step. The cabin crew expressed their gratitude and collected his information for the report. Crista also expressed her gratitude to him.

"If something similar were to happen to my nephew, I would want to be informed. There must be a witness who can assist," he expressed to her.

Chapter 9

When they arrived in Prague, the taxiing process took a bit longer than expected. Once they came to a stop, the main cabin crew politely requested that everyone remain seated. This was because the police needed to enter the plane. They had to remove a person before they could give permission for everyone to get off. Kenesta glanced at Crista. Her initial enthusiasm for the journey had vanished after the unfortunate incident. It left her yearning for solitude.

Crista grasped Kenesta's hand firmly. She knew they had to speak with the police before they could enjoy a private moment in the city. The rest of the flight was peaceful. The cabin crew quickly moved the person to a seat at the back of the plane. This action kept the young women safe and well. They could still sense the intensity of his gaze.

The cabin crew opened the doors and extended the stairs. They granted permission for the police and another person to board the aircraft. Meanwhile, the pilot emerged from the flight deck. The male cabin crew told them about the situation. The pilot looked a lot like a captain. He approached the girls and offered a sincere apology for the ordeal they had endured.

"Thank you," Crista said. She was grateful and acknowledged the exceptional care of the cabin crew. They went above and beyond to ensure their comfort and well-being.

"That's great news. Despina is truly the best pursuer we could wish for," the captain remarked, beaming at both of the girls.

At that moment, two police officers approached the board. They asked the pilot about the whereabouts of the person they had been told about. The female cabin crew, Despina, informed them of the seat assignment. One of them went with the male cabin crew to the assigned seat. The other stayed standing and asked Despina and the pilots about the situation. They sought info on any potential witnesses.

The passenger sitting across from the girls raised his hand. Two other passengers nearby did the same. The police officer arrived and took their statement. He got the details from the very start. Then, the officer turned to Crista. He bombarded her with a series of questions about the incident. She recounted the events to him. He nodded and turned to Kenesta, who avoided eye contact. Crista then explained to the officer that she was feeling uneasy. This was her first experience with discrimination.

The officer acknowledged the information and jotted it down. However, he advised Crista that she may need to provide a statement since it concerned her too. Crista promised she would, but she needed some time to fulfil her commitment. Therefore, the officer advised her to visit the office at her convenience. He informed them that any office in the Czech Republic would suffice, as long as it belonged to the state police.

Crista agreed and assured them that they would be there. The officer then turned to the captain and engaged in a conversation with him in Czech. Perhaps he was telling them what to do next. They were still getting off the plane and had yet to reach their destination. Despina graciously took the interphone. With an announcement, she granted passengers permission to leave the aircraft.

The crowd rose to their feet, gathering their belongings and departing. Crista glanced at Kenesta before rising to her feet and retrieving their bags.

"Kenesta, we can leave for now," she messaged her.

Kenesta gazed at her with a bittersweet smile before rising to her feet. She grabbed one of the bags and placed it on her back. Crista flashed a warm smile and gently took hold of her hand. She wanted to convey her unwavering support and presence for her.

"Thank you and I hope you have a wonderful stay here. I truly wish it exceeds your expectations," Despina said sincerely.

Crista expressed her gratitude before they departed from the plane and made their way to the bus. The passengers who extended their hands reached out and offered their well wishes. Crista hoped that these gestures would help. But Kenesta didn't seem to notice them.

On the bus to the terminal, Kenesta avoided eye contact with Crista. They held hands. Crista pondered on ways to bring joy back into Kenesta's life. She didn't recognise the person. She longed for the return of the cheerful and lively Kenesta.

The bus deposited them at the entrance. They ascended the stairs to reach passport control. From there, they made their way outside the security area and into the public space. Crista used to consider using public transport, such as buses and the underground. However, she now had doubts about this choice.

Crista glanced at her mobile phone and realised it was nearly lunchtime. She decided to grab a bite to eat. Then, she would go into the city centre to explore the places Kenesta had in mind.

"Are you interested in having a meal?"

Kenesta simply nodded and gestured towards the nearby KFC. Crista flashed a warm smile, and the two of them strolled over to their destination. They confidently placed an order for a single bucket, meant to be shared between the two of them. They settled at a table, savouring their meal in peaceful silence. Crista contemplated talking to Kenesta about the recent events. She wanted to know if Kenesta understood what to do. However, she was reluctant to upset her more. She was already in turmoil.

They finished their food. Then, they used public transit to reach the bustling city. From there, they strolled through the streets. They took in the sights and sounds of the city. Kenesta observed the people around her with curiosity, as she found herself in a new place. She was eager to see if the behaviour of the locals differed from what she was accustomed to in England. The language had a unique quality, different from English. Yet, she found it intriguing. She planned to ask Pav about learning some phrases once they returned to the UK.

After an hour of walking, they stumbled upon a river. As they approached the bridge, Kenesta noticed an eerie glow. It was coming from beneath it. She was curious to witness its true nature. She moved closer to the guardrail and peered under the bridge. But she failed to catch a glimpse of anything.

"Are you okay?" Crista inquired; her attention caught by Kenesta's leaning over the rail.

She asked about the odd lighting. She longed to uncover its mystery.

Crista glanced at her. She was trying to read the intensity of her gaze. But she found no trace of light in her eyes. "Do you believe in the power of magic?"

Kenesta nodded, noting the flickering nature of the phenomenon. It seemed to indicate the presence of wild magic or the casting of a spell.

It finally clicked for Crista. Kenesta could perceive enchanting pathways around her. They let her see the exact moment when her magic would be restored and with even more power. And just as she was about to let go, Kenesta vanished from the bridge.

Crista glanced around, hoping to go unnoticed. Fortunately, they went unnoticed by everyone. But now she was wondering where Kenesta disappeared.

Kenesta found herself unexpectedly transported beneath the bridge. Her magic took control without her permission. Beneath the bridge, she caught sight of a door, its faint glow emanating from within. Her eyes were transfixed as her hand reached out to the door, gently pushing it open with a slight creak. As Kenesta opened the door, a small room filled with people came into view. All eyes immediately turned towards her.

All the people held up sticks and aimed them at her. Kenesta was unfamiliar with whatever it was, but she was well aware of its potential to cause harm. She displayed her empty hands with utmost caution. She was hiding her magical abilities for now. Kenesta observed the individuals in the room. They wore clothes like those worn by her vampire companion in her world. The garments draped down to the floor, their deep blue hue adding a touch of mystery. A hood adorned each one, lending an air of intrigue to their appearance.

No one made the first move, despite an equal number of females and males present. All eyes were on Kenesta. She became the centre of attention. Everyone closely observed her every move. One of the men stepped forward and addressed her in an unfamiliar language. It wasn't Czech, the language she had heard from Pav and the people around her, nor was it English. It had some similarities to her native tongue. But there were still big differences.

The man unteres, "Kapanatutsa ele tu kelisiaa."

She gazed at him. She struggled to understand his words. This made her speak to him in her own language. She was curious about his response.

"Ceelistisa kosta elsia."

The people exchanged bewildered glances. They anticipated hearing many world languages. But their anticipation turned to astonishment. This happened when the girl before them began speaking a long-forgotten language. They may not have been language masters. But they knew the ancient tongue spoken by the long-departed elves.

Kenesta observed their perplexity and pondered whether they comprehended her words. However, met with silence, she attempted to communicate in English.

"Who is this?"

The people appeared even more perplexed. Perhaps they assumed she lacked the ability to communicate in any of their languages.

"May I inquire about your identity and the manner in which you arrived at this location?" The man inquired once again.

"Hi there, I Kenesta I see magic and teleport there, who you?" She responded in her fractured English.

"We belong to the Moonlight Order. You seem to be from another realm, don't you?"

"No, I appear here from Kelestia, don't know how."

"How did you learn English?" The man looked more interested in her.

"My soulmate teaches me," she answered.

"Soulmate?" Kenesta just nodded at his question. She didn't know how to tell him about her goddess. Her goddess appeared to her and told her this.

"I seek assistance. I need find a way to stay with her," she said instead.

"Is it possible for you to bring your soulmate here?" He asked her, and she nodded.

With closed eyes, she allowed her thoughts to drift towards Crista, longing to be in her presence. She had never used this teleportation method before. But she knew its mechanics well. She learned from her grandmother in her childhood.

Crista materialised beside her, looking disoriented. She surveyed her surroundings. She noticed a group of people clutching their sticks. But they were not aiming them in any particular direction.

"That's Crista," Kenesta remarked.

"Hi," Crista said. Her confusion was clear as she glanced at Kenesta. Kenesta seemed completely at ease with the other people.

"Hello, Crista. Kenesta mentioned that she wants to stay with you. But she said her English skills are not very strong. Perhaps you could help us translate a few things for her," the man said. He had been speaking throughout the conversation. He turned towards Crista.

She expressed her willingness to give it a shot.

"What have you gotten yourself into?" Crista gazed at Kenesta and silently conveyed her thoughts.

Kenesta gazed at her with a gentle smile, radiating innocence. She kept her trip's reason a secret. But, when she met someone with magical knowledge, her face lit up with joy.

"Sure," the man said with a smile, "do you happen to know how Kenesta came into this dimension? We need to understand how we can assist her."

"Well, I know about it. But I must admit, I am not entirely sure how it happened," Crista said. She was captivating her audience with the tale of the mirror and her discovery of Kenesta.

"Maybe we ought to move to a nicer place," the man suggested. He looked at the others. He spoke in the same language as before. He gave them a message that made everyone vanish. "If you could kindly accompany me, please."

Crista gazed at Kenesta, unsure of how to respond. They found themselves in an unknown land. They faced the daunting task of helping a complete stranger. Kenesta disliked the idea. But she wasted no time and promptly followed the man. He led her to the door on the opposite side of the room.

"I'm not so sure about that, Kenesta. We don't really know him, after all."

"Everything will be alright, please come."

"We are concerned about the actions he might take against us. He might take them because we lack weapons."

"You simply don't. I can overcome him, should he attempt anything."

Uncertain and hesitant, Crista remained rooted to the spot where she had materialised. She couldn't bring herself to venture anywhere with this man, as she felt a distinct unease.

"Don't worry, everything will be fine. I can ensure our safety by teleporting us if needed. Crista nodded in agreement and cautiously trailed behind Kenesta and the mysterious individual."

They trailed behind him as he made his way down the corridor, eventually arriving at yet another door. Just beyond them was a cosy sitting room. It was adorned with four inviting armchairs around a round table. The walls were adorned with shelves brimming with books.

"Please have a seat," the man gestured towards the armchairs. "Can I get you something to drink?"

"Just water for me," Crista said, settling into one of the plush armchairs.

"Me too," Kenesta exclaimed as she eagerly leapt into the armchair to the left of Crista.

The man easily floated three glasses of water to the table. He placed them in front of him and then sat down gracefully in another chair.

"Apologies, but would you mind providing an introduction? It seems you're already familiar with our names," Crista requested.

"Apologies for my oversight. I am Quentiss," he declared, his voice carrying the weight of authority. "As the leader of the Moonlight Order, I bear the responsibility of guiding our path."

"Do you possess magical abilities?" Crista inquired about Kenesta's activities, as she was curious to find out.

"Indeed, one could argue that I possess magical abilities. However, the accurate term to use is magus. I suppose Kenesta must be an elf."

"Yeah," Kenesta nodded. Her face was filled with pride as she showed her elegant, pointed ears. "How did you come to know?"

"The language you spoke has been dead for a long time. There are still some books written in it, but no one alive today can speak that language."

He then told them the captivating tale of the Moonlight Order. He described the enchanting realm of magic within their world. Kenesta had some questions. They were about the differences between the magic of this world and the magic she was used to back home. Quentiss shared with them the magical population's fascinating beliefs. This left Kenesta pleasantly surprised. She learned that they still devotedly worshipped her goddess alongside many others.

"Can you assist Kenesta?" Crista asked at the end.

"We can certainly give it a try, but I can't make any promises since I'll need to do some research first. I must admit, the concept of travelling between dimensions is completely new to me."

"It's okay." Crista kindly offered, "I can give you my contact information. Use it if you come across anything."

"That's a great idea," he agreed, nodding. They both reached for their mobile phones and exchanged numbers. Kenesta glanced around at the books, taking in the literary landscape. Crista noticed the expression on their face and made the decision to inquire.

"Could you please show Kenesta the books written in her language?"

With a casual wave of his hand, he beckoned a couple of books from the shelves. Kenesta gazed at them, her eyes drawn to the familiar alphabet. With a sense of curiosity, she reached out and selected one, flipping through its pages.

Crista observed her with a smile, aware of Kenesta's deep affection for books. Quentiss observed her with curiosity, eager to discover the contents of those books.

"Crista, this concerns the rich history of my people." Kenesta eagerly anticipated reading a book about magic in her native language. Crista couldn't help but burst into laughter upon hearing Kenesta's thoughts.

"Calm down, dear, you seem quite agitated," she messaged her.

Kenesta glanced up from the book, a mischievous smile playing on her lips. Crista recognised the look—Kenesta was a true bookworm, determined to devour every book in sight.

"I apologise for her behaviour," Crista said, turning to Quentiss.

"That's perfectly fine," he casually dismissed, waving his hand.

Crista acknowledged his words. She thought about the best way to get Kenesta out of the room. Then, they could go back to their hotel or keep exploring the city. But soon enough, she began to inquire about Quentiss and society he presided over. She wanted to delve deeper into his view of magic. Maybe she could learn to help Kenesta feel at ease using it in public.

They chatted for two hours. Then, Kenesta glanced up from her books. She asked if she could take them to the hotel and return them before their return to England. Quentiss hesitated, unsure if it was a wise decision. The books held immense value, both in age and significance. However, in the end, he relented. But, Kenesta would have to handle them with care and ensure their preservation.

Kenesta expressed her thanks. With Crista, she left the series of connected chambers. Outside, Kenesta gently grasped Crista's hand and transported them back to the bridge. They made their way to the hotel, both in need of some rest. Kenesta eagerly looked forward to delving back into their books.

In their room, Kenesta began delving into one of the books she had received from Quentiss. The focus was on her enchanting abilities. She knew some of the content. But she found new information that interested her. It made her more eager to delve deeper into the subject.

Crista went to the reception desk. She wanted to ask about a good restaurant for the two of them. The receptionist was kind. She mentioned a few nearby places. They were popular among both locals and tourists. He also cautioned her about tourist traps in the city. He advised her to avoid a particular restaurant.

Crista expressed her gratitude and armed with a map of the locations; she made her way back to the room. She noticed Kenesta on the bed, engrossed in a book. She felt the need to unwind. She had just had a stressful flight and an unexpected encounter. So, she chose to indulge in a soothing shower.

In the shower, her mind wandered to the events. She found herself reflecting on Despina, a member of the cabin crew.

She exuded genuine warmth that was truly refreshing. Perhaps it was time for a career change. She toiled in the restaurant for a long time. She harboured a deep disdain for her work. However, she strongly disliked it. But she couldn't find the courage to leave. She was gripped by fear and uncertainty. However, this cabin crew had sparked her. They motivated her to pursue a childhood dream. However, it would be great if Kenesta could also participate. Her fear of being alone resurfaced.

That also led her to realise that Kenesta was searching for a way to return to her own world. She was deeply unsettled by the thought of Kenesta departing from her in this world. If it were possible, she would accompany her. She lacked the enchantment necessary to endure in that place.

"I finally found it!" Kenesta sent her message with great enthusiasm.

"What did you find?" Crista asked. Then she left the shower and dried herself.

"The solution to my problem."

Her heart sank. It seemed that she would be returning soon. Crista emerged from the bathroom. She tried to seem excited about the latest news. But, deep down, she was consumed by despair.

"When elf find their mates, they can pass their abilities to them. Or they take their mates. So, you can have magic like me," she smiled at her.

"So, I can have magic like you?" She didn't know if she understood correctly.

"Yes," Kenesta nodded. She looked like a small kid during Christmas.

"And then could we stay together?"

"Yes, I could stay here with you. Learn languages, work and live our lives together."

"That would be nice. But I know you want to go home; you have to miss all your family and friends."

"I do, but I would be happy to live here with you, than in my world without you. And maybe there is a way I could visit them."

"Okay, we'll speak about it with Quentiss if he finds something if not, we'll continue to look for the answer."

"Thanks, Crista."

Crista smiled at her and changed into something comfortable. She was happier but still scared that Kenesta would change her mind and she'd lose her one day.

"Also, I was thinking, I will quit my job and apply for cabin crew in some airlines, what do you think?"

"Sounds good, do you think I can do it too? I really like the feeling and the cabin crew were so nice to us."

"Yes, we can apply together, but you need more practice in English," Crista said aloud.

"No problem, Kisti silista Entisa," Kenesta said and waved her hand around her head.

"Now, I speak fluent English, without more learning. Also, can learn another language without much trying. I can do the same for you if you want."

"Wow, I didn't know there was a spell like this," Crista was surprised. She was used to Kenesta's grammatical mistakes. It was nice to hear her with a British accent.

"Me neither, I found it in this book," she showed her the book of elf's spells.

Kenesta graciously shared with her a set of useful spells. Then, they both decided it was time to indulge in a delightful dinner. Crista picked a restaurant that specialised in Czech food. She and Kenesta were eager for a culinary adventure. As they entered, they saw Despina, a cabin crew member they had met earlier that morning. They were taken aback, yet they refrained from approaching her. They opted for a table tucked away in the far corner.

The waiter approached their table. They wasted no time ordering drinks. Crista, one of the Czech lagers, was on offer, and Kenesta decided to order a drink called Kofola. The waiter promptly delivered their order. As they looked at the menu, Despina approached their table.

"Hey ladies, how are you doing?" She said, a warm smile gracing her face as she looked at them.

"Uh, hi," Kenesta looked up from the menu when she heard her voice.

"It is better now, thanks. Did you have any problems after the incident?" Crista smiled at her and showed her to take a seat by their table.

"No, after the police left, we continued as if nothing happened and later, we just wrote the report. I just wanted to see if you feel better now that you rested a little bit," she said and sat for a bit.

"Yeah, we are much better now. Are you living here for a long time? Can you recommend us something?" Kenesta asked her.

"Of course, I could recommend the cream sauces. It's one of the best here. The potato pancakes are good," she smiled and pointed to the menu. Kenesta thanked her. When the waiter came back, she ordered the potato pancakes with chicken and veggies. Crista ordered the cream sauce. Despina stood by their table for another couple of minutes. Then, she returned to her friends.

Kenesta took a sip from a glass of black liquid, which looked like coke, but the taste was more flowery and less sweet. She liked it.

"Can we buy some home?" She asked Crista. Crista looked at her with surprise. Kenesta usually didn't like coke or over-sweet drinks.

"I guess. Maybe we can look if can find a Czech or Polish store that sells it."

"Okay," Kenesta smiled and took another sip.

After twenty minutes, another waiter brought their food, and they started eating. Kenesta looked at the potato pancakes. They looked good. But they were too oily and heavy for her. However, the sauce Crista had looked delicious. It was yellow, almost orange in colour and it was white bread and a piece of meat.

"Can I try?" Kenesta asked.

"Of course, if I can try yours."

Kenesta picked up her fork and knife. She sliced a small piece of bread. Then, she drizzled some sauce on it, experimenting with different flavours. The flavours of carrot and beef danced on her palate. There were hints of lemon, cream, and parsley as well. However, all things considered, it was truly excellent. Crista sampled her food. They continued to savour the food they had ordered.

The pancake turned out to be quite decent in the end. The flavours were delicious. The mix of tomato and chicken was perfectly balanced.

"Are we still planning on going to České Budějovice tomorrow?" Crista inquired once they had completed their meal.

"Yes, it is already planned. The train and the hotel are paid for. So, it would be only right to stick to our original plan," Kenesta nodded. She felt a surge of joy upon discovering the group that day. However, her curiosity beckoned her to explore the possibility of another city. Having multiple options is always preferable to being limited to just one.

Crista smiled, expressing her satisfaction. She felt a surge of joy when Kenesta expressed her desire to proceed with the plans. She may be hesitant to cover the cost of another hotel. They could consider going to a different city instead of Prague.

Chapter 10

The following morning, they found themselves rising early once again. This time, it was around five in the morning, as they had to catch a train departing at half past eight. They decided to grab a quick bite to eat before hopping on the train.

Last night, they took another stroll through the city, eager to catch a glimpse of the sunset. The old city was a breathtaking sight, bathed in the warm hues of the setting sun. Kenesta loved every moment with Crista in this strange land. She yearned for more exploration. Perhaps even exploring various countries and destinations.

They left the hotel. They asked for the fastest way to reach the train station. The receptionist kindly directed them to the underground. She also gave instructions on where to disembark. They followed the instructions. They reached the train station an hour before departure.

First, they surveyed their surroundings. They searched for signs or displays. The signs could show train info and directions to the platforms. After that, they began to search for a cute coffee shop. They wanted a place to enjoy a lovely breakfast. Fortunate circumstances led them to a bustling station. It was adorned with many charming coffee shops.

After careful thought, they settled on a delightful establishment. It boasted an array of tasty French pastries.

Kenesta decided to indulge in a delicious ham and cheese croissant. They also treated themselves to a mouth-watering crispy baguette topped with dry ham. They both also grab a cup of coffee and purchase a box of macaroons for the train ride. They settled down at a table, savouring their breakfast spread of food and coffee.

They eagerly awaited the train. They hoped it would come soon. Time was running out. They focused on finding the right platform and getting ready to start their journey. Crista took on the job of examining the train display. She carefully searched for the correct one based on her knowledge about the train.

When she stumbled upon it, they discreetly followed a group. The group was making their way towards the platforms. The process of establishing the platform was quite straightforward. Each platform was conveniently numbered. All of them had a board showing the train that would depart from there.

Upon arriving at the platform, Kenesta got the details of their reservation. They did this to find their assigned seat. Arriving a few minutes early was crucial. The train only stopped briefly. Although the train had not yet arrived, it was wise to be prepared.

As the train pulled in, they eagerly stepped on board and quickly located their seats. Kenesta settled into her seat by the window. Her curiosity was piqued by the pretty countryside of Czechia. Eager to soak in the sights, she yearned to witness every bit of its beauty. Crista settled into the aisle seat, ticket in hand, ready to present it to the contractor.

The journey lasted approximately three hours, with only a few brief stops along the way. Kenesta loved the experience. She even talked with a few local girls who overheard their English. They were inspired to practice their own language skills. Kenesta was filled with anticipation and joyfully engaged in conversation with them. They shared stories about their time in the Czech Republic. Kenesta mentioned her time living in the Kingdom. But she accidentally left out its name.

Crista chuckled softly. Kenesta was talking about a topic unrelated to the British Islands. However, Crista was truly intrigued by Kenesta's vast knowledge. It was about the British royal family and their complex affairs. Perhaps she shouldn't let Kenesta watch TV alone anymore.

"So, you want to move here?" One of the girls asked after a brief pause.

Kenesta responded with a smile, "I would love to, but unfortunately, it's not within my control." She then glanced over at Crista.

"We'll see," Crista replied. She was thinking about the chance of getting a job as a cabin crew member. She would submit her application in the evening. She was full of hope for success and acceptance.

The girl flashed a smile in their direction before diverting her attention to her phone. Kenesta glanced at Crista. She sensed that Crista had a secret. Kenesta felt a surge of excitement.

As they stepped off the train, their eyes were drawn to the map. Eager to explore, they planned to visit the nearby square and realised it was also close to lunchtime. Kenesta, in her role as the leader, took it upon herself to guide them. Unfortunately, they ended up taking a wrong turn at the next junction they were meant to follow. They found themselves not at the square, but near the river. They had a pretty view of the countryside.

Crista chuckled, declaring her refusal to let the other person take the lead again. They retraced their steps along the familiar path. Eventually, they stumbled upon the square. The area was quaint, bustling with a variety of shops and restaurants. There stood a statue in the middle of the square.

The girls had a delightful day. They explored the town, took strolls, and admired the tourist attractions. When it came time to head to their accommodation, they proceeded at a leisurely pace. They weren't seeking the magical community. But Kenesta noticed a few subtle signs of magic around them. Deep down, they knew that going into the woods would likely lead them to encounter vampires. They might also meet other supernatural beings. And she desired to visit the place during the evening when Crista would be peacefully sleeping.

In the hotel, Crista insisted on inspecting the room first. But Kenesta's growling stomach urged her to go to the restaurant for an early dinner. In the end, they reached a compromise. They put their things in the room and went out for dinner.

In the evening, they retired to their room and enjoyed a relaxing movie marathon. Meanwhile, Crista submitted two applications. They were for cabin crew positions at Lynx Airline's Prague base. The applications were submitted for both of them. But she had to embellish Kenesta's CV and some of her past work to improve their chances.

At ten in the evening, Crista drifted off to sleep. Kenesta found herself at the edge of the forest. There, she felt a strong magic. The magic felt familiar, reminiscent of the one she knew from her home. The atmosphere remained unchanged. This was true when she visited her vampire friend or was at her own house.

She pondered. Were the creatures in the forest the same as those in the realm of magic? She ventured into the depths of the forest. She wandered aimlessly, longing for a chance encounter with another soul. After hours of walking, she found herself unsuccessful in her pursuit. Frustrated, she made the decision to rely on her magical abilities to guide her path.

With a flick of her wrists, she released the enchanting power. It guided the mystical creatures to their destination. She soon stumbled upon a small village that bore a striking resemblance to her own. Standing on the outskirts of the village, she surveyed her surroundings. If she didn't know any better, she might have mistaken her surroundings for home. However, upon closer inspection, she noticed a few distinct differences. For instance, the roads here were made of rocks. Back home, they were made of sand.

As she scanned her surroundings, a sense of unease washed over her. Suddenly, she detected a presence closing in from behind. In a split second, she raised her guard. She was protecting herself from a threat. In a fleeting moment, her shield appeared. It absorbed the curse with ease before vanishing.

Kenesta glanced over her shoulder. She saw a man who looked a lot like her father. He looked very similar. He had dark blond hair and matching facial features. These features included his nose and eyes. He stared at her in astonishment, caught off guard by her sudden act of self-defence. But when he gazed upon her, even he could discern resemblances to himself.

"May I inquire about your identity?" He spoke in her native language.

Kenesta was surprised by the news. This was true because Quentiss had assured her before that she was truly unique.

She introduced herself to him as Kenesta. She was the daughter of Mikista. This was her custom in her world.

The man couldn't conceal his astonishment upon hearing her speak in the same language. He knew he could travel between worlds. But he was not expecting to meet his brother's daughter.

"My name is Kilistas, welcome Kenesta," he said in a much warmer and friendlier tone than before.

Kenesta was taken aback by the name. Her father mentioned her uncle Kilistas. But they hadn't planned on visiting him. He lived on the other side of Okolesta. That was complete nonsense, considering they could have effortlessly teleported there.

"I can sense your thoughts, my dear niece," Kilistas said, catching her off guard with his choice of address.

"But how?" She wasn't sure how to complete her thought. She had too many questions about this situation.

"How am I here? Or how had we never met?" he helped her to formulate her thoughts and she nodded. These were some of the questions she had.

"I will answer it, but first tell me how you appeared here?"

"Well, I am not really sure. But Crista told me that she saw me in the mirror. When she touched it, I appeared on the floor of her work," Kenesta said.

"Well, I'm not sure. But, according to Crista, she said she saw my reflection in the mirror. When she touched it, I materialised on her workplace floor," recounted Kenesta.

"Ah, a timeless tale of soul mates," Kilistas smiled warmly, "how about we find a cosy spot to chat? There is so much I want to share with you, my dear niece."

Kenesta nodded in agreement and followed Kilistas to one of the houses. They settled into plush armchairs, ready to engage in a deep conversation. Kenesta asked about the community in the forest. Kilistas responded, "It's a safe space for elves, like us." Sometimes, people find peace in leaving civilisation. They seek a space where they can truly be themselves. In these secluded realms, however, one often discovers a lack of permanent inhabitants.

He asked Kenesta about her experiences since her arrival. She then told a story about her encounter with Crista. She also said she believed she had lost her magical powers. She shared with him her English language journey. She also told him about their adventurous trip to the Czech Republic. There, they sought help to get home or to learn how to spread joy.

Kilistas chuckled at her weak English. Then, she resorted to her magic. He explained that it was common for their magic to be used up. This happened after travelling between dimensions in search of their soulmate. It would take a few weeks, if not months, for their powers to fully recharge. He ceased his laughter as soon as Kenesta shared the news about Quentiss.

"Be cautious when dealing with this individual. He is cunning. He constantly seeks to exploit us for his own research or world domination schemes. If he contacts you again, kindly tell him that you made the hard choice to give up magic to be with Crista."

She nodded in agreement. It was logical. He was very eager to help her. He made a real effort to build a warm and friendly bond. Crista was spot on when she expressed her reservations about him.

"Sure, I'd be happy to exchange numbers with you so we can keep in touch. Feel free to reach out if you have any more questions. Yet, it seems that the hour is growing late, and it would be wise for you to retire for the night."

"Can you assure me that we will keep in contact?" She asked him.

"Certainly, I give you my word. You all mean the world to me, and I'm excited to introduce you to my husband and kids," he said with a smile.

"Do you have children?"

"Yes, thanks to our great abilities, I got to feel the joy of having a biological child," he said with a smile. He shared the story of his husband and their three kids. Kenesta eagerly anticipated the day she would finally meet them.

She eventually went to their hotel room. She settled in for a good night's rest. She knew that tomorrow would be busy. In the morning, they had to make their way back to Prague before catching their flight back home. Kenesta had no desire to leave this country. She found great pleasure in this place.

They started their day with a great breakfast at the hotel restaurant. They savoured the delicious flavours before going to the train station. Their train was scheduled to leave at 10:30. They made their way to the station, ready to start their next adventure. Kenesta remained silent about her evening escapade to Crista. She was unsure of how to confess because she had gone behind her back.

"Is everything okay?" Crista inquired, noticing her sudden tranquillity.

"Yes, I was recently pondering about this upcoming journey. I have serious doubts about Quentiss," she remarked. She was reluctant to disclose the reasons or the process behind her realisation.

"Thank goodness. The man gives me an unsettling feeling."

"Yeah, I feel the same way. Perhaps I was too hasty in placing my trust in him," Kenesta agreed with a nod.

"It's good that you've come to that realisation," Crista said with a smile as she gently kissed her on the forehead.

"I share in the joy," Kenesta said with a smile. She gracefully shifted the conversation to a more relaxed topic. When they return home, they can share their plans and discuss their job search.

Crista reassured her that they would find something. She also mentioned that she had already applied for the cabin crew job in Prague. And even if only one of them understood, they would still stick together. Kenesta was overjoyed to hear the news. Her love for this country grew even stronger when she discovered that one of her uncles was living here. It only fuelled her desire to stay.

During their train journey, they talked about the preparations. These were in case they got in and had to move. Kenesta was anxious about their finances. But Crista reassured her they had nothing to worry about. Crista assured Kenesta. They had enough money to support themselves for a few years without work. She said she would pay for their accommodation.

Kenesta agreed with a nod. But she made it clear that once she started earning, she would pay half of the rent. She felt it was important not to let Crista bear the financial burden alone.

"I sense that our conversation revolves primarily around this topic. Kenesta, believe me. I love pampering you. You don't need to worry about paying," Crista sighed.

"I don't want to rely on you, and I also want to treat you well," Kenesta smiled.

During the train journey, they were able to check in for their flight that evening. They wondered if the crew on the flight would be the same as two days ago or if there would be new faces. But most of all, they prayed that no one would harbour prejudice against the LGBTQ+ community.

"Once we reach Prague, would you be interested in exploring the museum? We have about six hours before we need to head to the airport." Just before they arrived in Prague, Crista asked Ken about the last hour.

"Sure, I can do that. Why not?" She nodded.

Crista smiled. She eagerly reached for her phone to buy tickets for the national museum.

Kenesta smiled warmly at her, a glimmer of anticipation in her eyes. With grace, she took her phone from her pocket. She quickly sent a message to Kilistas. This would give him her contact information. She thanked them again for the warning. Then, she asked if she could visit her family.

It took a few minutes before he responded, but he sent her a ritual that she could use to travel between dimensions. He cautioned her against excessive use as it would deplete her magical energy. After each journey, she required a day or two of rest before returning. She made a promise to him, assuring him that she wouldn't abuse her power. She empathised with his worries. She saw the importance of not relying only on her magic. But she feared the consequences of being helpless without it.

In Prague, they opted to stroll to the museum instead of taking the crowded underground. The main train station was close. It was convenient. This made it a pleasant and time-saving choice. They made a beeline for the electronic ticket tourniquets in the museum.

Kenesta loved history. She took in every portrait and attraction that adorned the surroundings. Crista purchased a brochure showcasing various destinations. They kept hushed. They were careful not to disrupt the serene museum. Yet, they relished every moment there. After four hours, they decided to eat. Then, they would leisurely take buses and the underground to the airport.

They proceeded directly to the passport control upon arrival at the airport. Kenesta was surprised. They didn't go straight to security when they arrived in Birmingham. Crista reassured her. They would need to pass them. It was a requirement for international travel.

None of the girls were interested in shopping at the duty-free shop. They felt that way after going through passport control. Instead, they began searching for their boarding gate. They went down the narrow path to the ground-level gates. But they found they would need to go through security before reaching the gate. To their dismay, there was no coffee shop in sight.

They made the decision to return to the first floor, where they casually strolled past a Costa Coffee. They opted to take a seat and unwind for a while before continuing on to the gate. Crista treated them to hot chocolate and a selection of pastries. Kenesta's excitement bubbled as they settled back into the plane. They patiently waited. They found solace by the window. They were captivated by the majestic aircraft. The aircraft represented various airlines.

"Could we perhaps embark on a few of those journeys in the future?" Kenesta asked Crista.

"Of course, we can arrange another trip far away," she said with a smile. She was eager.

"I'm filled with anticipation," Kenesta said, lost in her thoughts. She marvelled at the countless destinations that these planes were bound for.

After a lengthy flight, they finally touched down in Birmingham. They didn't waste any time. They swiftly navigated through passport control and went to the car.

Crista was behind the wheel while Kenesta peacefully dozed off as the night grew late. Crista relished the trip, yearning for its duration to stretch further. Alas, all good things must come to an end, and she found herself reluctantly returning to the realm of work.

As Crista embarked on her journey, her mind was consumed with thoughts of preparation. She pondered a new job. She saw herself being hired by the airline. If they found themselves in a different country or decided to stay in the UK. They were certain that relocation was inevitable, regardless of the circumstances. She might consider either renting or selling the flat. And then they can purchase or lease a new one near their home airport.

The airline took nearly two weeks to respond. But, in the end, they were both invited to interview in Bristol on one of the open days. Crista diligently dedicated herself to her work throughout the past fortnight.

Kenesta stayed home. She kept in touch with her new uncle. Their conversations gave her valuable insights. They were about their shared heritage and his family history. Her excitement grew. She prepared to see her beloved cousins and the enchanting earth elves. She received a few messages from Quentiss during this time. But she always dodged his questions about the books he had loaned her. She often insisted that the books were nothing more than stories for children.

Every time he reached out to her, Kenesta would contact her uncle. He would reassure her that he would lose interest if she didn't give him any useful information.

During her lunch break, Crista received an email from the company. As she sat down to savour her meal, she couldn't help, but glance at her phone, particularly her email. And there it was; the email she had been anxiously anticipating.

As she began to read the email, she was taken aback by the unexpected content. She was caught off guard by their decision to invite both of them. She would be fine if they invited either Kenesta or her alone. They wanted to talk to both people. They might invite them to join the training.

She carefully read the email. She paid close attention to the details of the upcoming open day. She made sure to note the time and place where they were invited to participate. Right away, she recognised her duty to meet her work obligations. She saw she would have to ask for time off to do so.

She scanned the room, searching for her manager. He found himself perched on the bar. With a sudden surge of excitement, she rose from her chair and hurried towards him.

"Sure, may I have a moment of your time to talk?"

"Of course, is everything okay?" He gazed at her with concern.

"Yes, indeed. But I need Wednesday off if that is possible?"

He agreed to check, assuring her that everything should be in order. They walked over to his computer, where he had their work schedule and bookings.

The manager carefully examined the day. Three more girls on the roster could handle the bookings well. They made Crista's presence unnecessary.

"Indeed, this has potential. Next time, please tell me earlier," he said quietly. He removed Crista from his plans for that day.

"Unfortunately, I just received an email informing me that I have to be somewhere else. But thank you," Crista said with a smile as she returned to her partially consumed sandwich.

During her meal break, she talked to Kenesta. They discussed the upcoming open day and the needed preparations. They needed to go shopping. Kenesta didn't have any professional clothes. They were needed for the open-day grooming.

Kenesta received a message from Crista while she was at home. As she read it, a surge of excitement filled her. She dreamed of working and exploring new countries. She couldn't help it. She let her imagination run wild. She envisioned the things she would bring and the fun places they would explore.

Crista also sent her a text. It mentioned that they should go shopping for professional clothes. Kenesta was unsure of the meaning of her words. But her excitement for the shopping trip was clear. Now she just had to wait for Crista to return from work. She was eager for the moment they could start their shopping spree for the big occasion.

Kenesta couldn't sit still for the rest of the day. She felt an urge to take action. So, she made a spontaneous decision to go to the library to check if Pavlina was there. Unfortunately, the girls were absent. So, Kenesta decided to leave after a few minutes. She strolled through the busy city streets. Her gaze was drawn to the captivating displays in the shop windows. She had some remaining funds from Crista, but she was reluctant to exhaust them all.

While on her stroll, she stopped at an ice cream parlour. She had a refreshing bowl of frozen yoghurt there. It was adorned with many tasty fruits. With her sweet treat in hand; she resumed her leisurely amble down the bustling High Street. She continued until she reached the end of the street. The small square stood in stark contrast to the grand cathedral that faced it.

The stunning architecture captivated Kenesta. It made her decide to step inside. After navigating the bustling streets, she found herself standing by the main doors. From that spot, the cathedral appeared even grander. It looked even better than from far away.

She entered the room as the door beckoned her with its open invitation. The sight of the towering ceiling and the sturdy pillars caught her off guard. Kenesta was filled with awe as she took in the vast expanse of space before her. Curiosity consumed her. She yearned to delve deeper into its history and construction. Unfortunately, there was no one available to satisfy her thirst for knowledge. Undeterred, she started a solitary journey. She traced the walls' perimeter, carefully examining every tiny detail.

As she reached another set of doors, they opened. They revealed a beautiful garden woven with a peaceful churchyard. She strolled around, taking in every detail, her eyes eager to capture as much as possible. And then, amidst the bustling streets, a quaint little shop caught her attention. It was filled with an array of delightful souvenirs. She arrived at the destination and purchased a book centred around the cathedral.

Kenesta found a quiet spot on a bench along the walls and immersed herself in a book. The cathedral was serene and still. It surrounded her in the rich tapestry of its storied past. She experienced a profound sense of tranquillity and serenity in this particular setting.

As she read for a few minutes, she couldn't help but wonder. Why hadn't she come here sooner? Its beauty and warm hospitality made her feel right at home. She hoped a similar haven awaited her. They were bound for unfamiliar territory.

The cathedral was hushed. It stirred many thoughts in Kenesta's mind. She was the subject of divine contemplation. Recently, she has been dedicating a significant amount of time to meditation. Throughout the day, she thanked her multiple times for the chance to be with Crista. However, she couldn't shake the nagging sensation that her efforts were insufficient. She felt a deep sense of gratitude yet found herself at a loss for words.

"You are under no obligation to take any action." A gentle breeze slipped through the open window, whispering like a divine presence. The air seemed to grow warmer, enveloping me in a comforting embrace. Kenesta could feel it, a sudden jolt coursing through her body. She clutched the book tightly. But it slipped from her grasp and crashed onto the floor with a thud.

The few people at the cathedral looked at her. A book fell with a loud thud. Its impact echoed in the quiet space.

"Is everything okay, miss?" An older woman approached cautiously. She gently guided Kenesta from shock to clarity, helping her understand her surroundings.

"Yeah, I apologise," she said as she swiftly retrieved the book from the floor.

"Don't worry, my dear. At times, the spirits here have a message. It can be surprising," the elderly woman reassured her before leaving.

Kenesta carefully observed the woman's posture. She gracefully made her way to the garden entrance. With a dismissive shake of her head, she made the firm decision to leave. She was puzzled by the events. She was determined to return before they left town.

On her journey back, her mind was consumed by the old lady's words and the divine guidance she had received. She felt compelled to thank the goddess. The goddess had assured her that no action was needed. And she had to contemplate the most effective approach. Maybe her uncle could lend her a helping hand.

As soon as she arrived home, she felt a strong urge to reach out to her uncle. But one of the books Quentiss had given her immediately captivated her. She hadn't read that book yet. But the title intrigued her: *Tradition of Elves and Their Beliefs*. She had the book in her hands. She eagerly flipped through the pages. Her eyes scanned for that one section about various rituals.

She found a piece that thanked a god. She found another about the act of supplication. She meticulously absorbed the content, finding it precisely tailored to her needs. However, before acting, she decided to ask her uncle for more assurance.

Kenesta spent the time until Crista got home on the phone with her uncle. They were discussing the best approach. He shared with her the details of his daily ritual. He described how it made him feel a sense of belonging. This feeling surpassed the grand ritual she had come across in her reading.

Kenesta was inspired by his example and began practising it too. To truly embrace the essence of the dawn, one must rise with the first light and venture outdoors. In order to witness the sunrise, she would need to locate a hill. As the sun emerged, she would thank the goddess three times. She would also offer prayers for a good day.

Chapter 11

The days after the email were hectic for Crista and Kenesta. Crista had to go to work. They also had to do errands and make resumes.

Never before had Kenesta felt such fear before a job interview. She was sure that if she messed up, she would be passed over. Crista assured her that all would be fine. But she had her doubts.

On her way to the open day, Kenesta sported a dark blue jacket and a dress shirt in sky blue. Black trousers, a white shirt, and a black jacket were Crista's choice of outerwear. Both of them were wearing high heels. Kenesta felt very out of place since she had never worn heels before.

She had never had the chance to wear one before because it did not exist in her society. Since Crista often wore her high heels to parties and even to work sometimes, they were second nature to her, especially if something significant happened.

They took the car to Bristol to visit the open day. Crista opted for a more casual shoe style for the car ride, ditching her heels in favour of flats. Upon arrival, she intended to undergo a transformation. She was watching out for herself because driving in high heels wasn't fun or safe.

The journey to Bristol was quick and trouble-free. Since the females weren't in the mood to chat, they sat around the radio. But Crista still needed to drive safely and legally. They had a fixation on their own ideas.

As they checked in for the open day, a throng of young people arrived. Many were dressed properly. They milled about the hotel lobby. Concern grew in Kenesta's eyes as she turned to Crista. She was nervous. She aspired to become completely invisible.

"Everything is going to be alright. We go there and do teamwork. We talk to the representatives. Then we go home," Crista mentally resurrected herself and continued.

At least in Kenesta's opinion, it was. Still, she was unconvinced by the size of the crowd that was waiting outside.

With a radiant smile on her face, Crista leaned in and passionately kissed her forehead.

After making a show of confidence, Kenesta finally said, "Okay, let's go."

They stepped out of the vehicle. They strolled hand in hand with the group of spectators.

"Hello, are you attending the open day today?" Crista inquired.

A handful of 'yeah' were the replies she got when she asked.

They chose to chat with other candidates before the recruitment day started. They did this so they would know each other better for team assignments.

As soon as it was time to begin, a few airline staff led them to a room with six enormous tables. They told them to find a seat at one of them. Crista and Kenesta chose one in the front.

During the first half an hour, they were introduced to each other and given the day's agenda. After the briefing, they were to do a team exercise. Then, they would move to separate rooms for interviews. Everyone else would take a break at the same time.

The team did an exercise. They had to think of ways to handle a disruptive passenger. They had to do it without taking matters into their own hands. It was a lot of fun even though Crista and Kenesta were on opposite teams. Crista's teammates were great. And their solution was simple. Kenesta, on the other side, had never encountered anyone as egotistical as her teammates. The situation would get much worse if they implemented their poor remedy.

Interviews began following the solutions' demos. In alphabetical sequence, they proceeded. They decided to grab some food because they were both at the very bottom of the list. Compared to Crista, Kenesta was the most anxious about the interview as a whole.

Crista did her best to reassure Kenesta. It was before her interview with the airline official. But Kenesta still couldn't relax. All she could think about was how disappointing it would be for Crista if she failed.

A separate room was summoned for Kenesta after she had waited for an hour. Before her departure, Crista embraced her and sent her best wishes. A middle-aged woman with spectacles and a head full of paperwork sat inside. Looking up from the papers, Kenesta stood up as soon as she stepped inside.

"Hello, I assume you're Kenesta?" The woman asked.

Kenesta stated, "Hi, yes that's me," before nodding.

"Hello, Kenesta. My name is Elizabeth and I work for the Lynx Airline. Please, have a seat," the woman added, gesturing towards the chair beside her table.

After saying 'thank you', Kenesta took a seat. The questions in typical interviews are like "Tell me about yourself." They also asked, "Why do you want to work for our airline?"

Kenesta did her best to be honest in her responses. When it was her turn to ask, she tried to come up with something she didn't know. She asked about their work hours. She asked if they could share a base with their partner. She asked about other similar topics.

She answered all of the interviewer's questions and the look on her face was one of admiration. While doing so, she jotted down some notes for the papers.

"Alright, Kenesta. If you have no further inquiries, you are free to go. After the last candidate finishes, we will tell you," Elizabeth informed her. Kenesta hurriedly thanked and departed from the room. On her return to the previous room, she searched far and low for Crista, but to no avail.

Kenesta was perplexed for a moment. She considered the chance that she was in another room and would return soon. Her throat felt as dry as the Sahara. She hurried to the refreshment table and drank from a glass of water.

"How many more people are there, in your opinion?" Kenesta was approached by a group of girls who were standing nearby.

After the last person was announced, another woman suggested taking a break. Then they could make a decision.

"Well, I certainly don't want to be the last one. The interviewer has probably heard so many other candidates. Your chances of getting it are slim," another woman added.

"Yeah, they're tired. And they're completely ignoring these people," the first woman said.

Kenesta sat down in her chair to await Crista's arrival, interrupting their chat. These females wouldn't make decent team members if they continued to act that way, she thought. After waiting another five minutes, Crista approached her, beaming. But, upon seeing Kenesta, Crista embraced her and asked about her emotions.

She was honest when she informed her, "I think I did well. But some girls were saying that the last people are the least likely to get the job."

"It's not true. The changes in the first ones are actually identical to those in the last ones." As Crista gently pointed out, the interviewer had been taking notes the whole time. These notes would help in picking the best candidates.

"Is that so?" Kenesta inquired.

The word 'yes' came out of Crista's mouth with conviction.

Just ten minutes after they had taken their seats, they were summoned back. They probably already decided which candidates would continue in the hiring process.

It took about five minutes for everyone to return. Then, a recruiter told them to stand up and go to the front when their names were read. The recruiter continued to read the names from the list. Kenesta's anxiety rose because neither her nor Crista's names appeared.

Twenty names were read out of forty by the recruiter before they ended. They did not contain Crista or Kenesta.

The people whose names were taken were asked to pack and go and they were asked to "try next time." They then returned to their seats and gathered their belongings.

"To the rest of you, I want to congratulate you on making it thus far. To continue, please email us copies of your passport. Also, send your criminal records and employment references. Once you've completed all of this, we will tell you if and when we will send you to train. Or we will sadly stop our work with you. At this time, you are free to depart, and we eagerly await the emails with these documents."

They had accomplished it, and Kenesta smiled broadly at Christa. It was only a formality to send the documents. They passed the interview. She knew Crista would take care of it at home.

They said goodbye to the hotel with a shared smile as Crista returned the gesture. On the way to the car, Crista couldn't help but smile at Kenesta's irreverent antics. Kenesta danced joyfully around her. After overhearing their talk earlier, she could tell that the news had Kenesta all giddy.

On the way back to their house, they chatted excitedly and made plans for the future. The results excited Crista, but she was really just listening to Kenesta speak.

Midway through, Crista suggested that she could get in touch with her uncle. He was also waiting for the results.

Kenesta paused briefly while talking about the new flat. Then, she retrieved her phone to call her uncle. "True," she said.

At this point, her uncle jumped on the phone to find out how she was doing and whether or not it had been effective. Kenesta proceeded to tell him about their day and the interviewer. She did this while laughing off his impatience.